SPELL STREET SWING

SPELL STREET SWING

SCIONS OF MAGIC™ BOOK FIVE

TR CAMERON   MICHAEL ANDERLE   MARTHA CARR

DISRUPTIVE IMAGINATION

Copyright © 2020 TR Cameron & Michael Anderle
Cover Art by Jake @ J Caleb Design
http://jcalebdesign.com / jcalebdesign@gmail.com
Cover copyright © LMBPN Publishing
A Michael Anderle Production

LMBPN Publishing
PMB 196, 2540 South Maryland Pkwy
Las Vegas, NV 89109

First US edition, February 2020
Version 1.02, May 2020
ebook ISBN: 978-1-64202-764-8
Print ISBN: 978-1-64202-765-5

Thanks to the JIT Readers

Diane L. Smith
Dave Hicks
Larry Omans
Dorothy Lloyd
Nicole Emens
Jeff Eaton
Deb Mader

If I've missed anyone, please let me know!

Editor
Skyhunter Editing Team

For those who seek wonder around every corner and in each turning page. And, as always, for Dylan and Laurel.

— TR Cameron

CHAPTER ONE

Caliste Leblanc tripped over a protruding pipe and barely managed to stop herself before she toppled over the edge. The sight of the street three stories below triggered a spike of icy fear in her stomach. She crouched to catch her breath and cursed the setting sun for hiding the offending projection from view. Neither the fall nor the foul language was perhaps appropriate for the nineteen-year-old matriarch of House Leblanc, one of the nine noble houses of New Atlantis, but who gave a damn?

Tanyith Shale, ex-prisoner and her sometimes investigation and battle partner, laughed softly. "Graceful."

"Shut it." She pushed her long red curls out of her face and tucked them behind her ears. "This is all your fault, anyway."

He shook his head. In the last few weeks, he'd returned to the look he claimed was normal for him—brown hair buzzed on the sides and piled high on the top of his skull, jeans, t-shirt, hoodie, and big black army boots.

It looks good on him. She chuckled. *The elderly are so hip*

1

these days. In truth, he was only seven or eight years older than her. She could never remember which and it didn't really matter since he was essentially ancient either way.

His voice was low and he gestured to the street below. "We both wanted more information on the Atlantean gang's drug trade. So technically, it's also your fault."

"I'm not the one who's taking care of an errand for the Malniets."

"Okay, that's a fair point."

She grinned. "You're giving up awfully easy. It's not like you. Did Kendra tire you out or something?" She gave him an eyebrow waggle that suggested naughtiness.

He twisted his back as if to ease it. "No, but being sore all the time does. I don't know what I did to myself in New Atlantis, but it sucks."

"It could be anything. It was a long swim, plus the fight against the octopus." She shuddered at the memory. After the Kraken attack, she'd begun to dislike the sea creatures. Once the second massive tentacled beast targeted them, it had become an outright phobia.

"Sure. Anyway, they're moving."

Cali snapped her gaze to the people they were tracking. Three Atlantean gang members had taken a route to one of the streets that were a known distribution point for Shine, the drug they'd developed to entice humans in New Orleans. The black backpack on the lone female of the group appeared to be full of product.

Once the three had moved out of sight, she used a blast of force magic to launch herself to the next rooftop across the street and one story down. It wasn't an issue to allow them a small lead as the Draksa who had adopted her flew

2

above to keep an eye on things. When she thought of him, he delivered a flow of amusement over the magical channel that connected their minds.

"Don't get too full of yourself," she sent. "It's not like I chose you to be my life partner. That was all you." More mirth confirmed his understanding of her joke. The truth was, though, the pairing seemed like destiny or fate. Each day, their connection strengthened, although he still could only send emotion. She feared the moment when the dragon lizard would be able to actually respond with real words through this bond.

Tanyith landed on the black surface beside her and scattered small stones in a circle around him, but the soft sound was thankfully lost in the noise that filtered from the streets below. They darted across the roof and reacquired their targets. The road the gang members had moved onto was a one-way lane that ran parallel to the main routes. Even the bigger roadways at the fringes of the French Quarter weren't that big, although there was a fair amount of foot traffic—more than one would expect if they were unaware that it was essentially a shopping mall for illicit goods and services. Occasional cars parked on both sides of the street evidenced various states of disrepair.

"A shopping mall with a hot new store in town," she muttered under her breath as she watched the trio separate. The woman with the backpack took her position on the front steps of a house with black bars over the windows and a matching metal grate over the elegant entry door. One of the two men wandered up and down the street to interact with potential customers in what was clearly a well-practiced routine. The other lingered nearby to manage either money or delivery. "Don't they usually have another person?" she whispered.

Her partner nodded where he crouched beside her. "Yeah. They must have more business than they can handle if they've spread themselves this thin."

She shook her head. "And that is not good." They watched in silence for a quarter of an hour and mapped the flow of people and product. The shimmer of the Draksa's veil from the building across the way was occasionally visible and she wondered, as she usually did, whether everyone could see it or if she was merely especially attuned. Instead of asking Tanyith what was essentially an irrelevant question, she said, "How do you want to handle it? My thought is maximum chaos."

He laughed. "So, business as usual, then. Do you care to share a few more details?"

"Fyre comes out of hiding and flies over once to get people moving. On his return trip, he ices any of the Atlanteans still around." His frost breath was excellent for disabling enemies in a fight without killing them and locked them in a magically frozen shell. "We deal with any runners."

Tanyith shrugged. "It seems like as good a plan as any. I'm ready when you are."

Cali had sent her thoughts to the Draksa as she spoke and approval flowed back from him. *Of course, he's always happy to be the star.*

With another shake of her head, she banished the smile from her face and readied herself to leap. She was about to give the command for him to start the attack when the movement of the people inexplicably changed. "Hold on—what's going on?"

What had previously been two streams of pedestrians moving in opposite directions on either side of the street became twin flows away from the far end. The speed shifted from a saunter to a deliberate walk that would probably become a run. She squinted and finally located three men in the typical cheap-suit uniform of the Zatora crime syndicate's middle-level goons.

The current representatives also wore long trench coats that weren't appropriate to the weather but were perfectly suitable to hide weapons. Two wore black and the other tan. They didn't present an obvious threat that she could see, but something must have made the people decide that being somewhere else at the moment would be a better choice.

She nudged Tanyith. "Maybe they're ugly. Like, disfigured. What do you think?"

He sighed and shook his head, doubtless jealous over her immense wit. "Well, there's only one way to find out."

"Right. Attack them."

"Okay, make that two ways. I thought we'd wait for them to get closer."

"Honestly, you're no fun at all." She shook her head. "Fine. Have it your way." Many of those selling illegal goods followed their customers hastily in an effort to leave the area, and the Atlantean gang members joined the flow when the Zatoras had covered a quarter of the length of the street.

As soon as it became apparent that they had chosen flight rather than fight, a man called, "Hey. 'Lant freaks.

Take another step and we'll put you down." The three men raised weapons and aimed at their quarry. Two held rifles and the man in the middle with the tan coat brandished a shiny silver revolver that looked too large for his hand.

The Atlanteans stopped and turned to face the new arrivals. They were all empty-handed and obviously had brought no weapons, but their postures displayed little concern at the evident threat. The woman's voice rang out, contemptuous and confident. "Put your toys away and go home, humans." She shrugged the backpack into a more centered position on her back with a casualness that spoke arrogance and unconcern.

"Hey, boss, do you hear that?" one of the men in black coats replied. "I guess we'd better take off, huh?" He laughed in the way that only genuine bootlickers ever could.

The Zatora in the center twitched the revolver slightly as he nodded. "Yeah, we're probably no match for them. But maybe this once, we'll get lucky." It was the same voice that had spoken the first time and carried a heavy dose of contempt.

The Atlanteans' posture changed and became more rigid and tense. "This is insane," Cali whispered. "Force shields will block anything the Zatoras have and they will find themselves cooked, electrocuted, or otherwise obliterated." She shook her head. "We need to stop this from escalating any further."

Tanyith hissed his disgust. "Why? Let the scum wipe each other out." She twisted to glare at him and he seemed to realize what he'd said and shrugged. "How many risks can we take until we lose?"

Cali replied with a short laugh. "At least one more, I hope. Are you ready?" He nodded, and she sent the mental command to the Draksa as she said the words aloud. "Start it up, Fyre."

He unveiled and launched himself off his perch. The twilight glinted from his metallic scales, which had morphed over time into a mixture of platinum and gold. His body elongated and his legs tucked against his torso while his neck extended to balance the long heavy tail at the opposite end. He roared to attract the attention of all those below, and the Atlanteans summoned the expected force shields. The Zatoras jerked their weapons up in surprise and pulled the triggers reflexively.

The creature dipped and wove deftly to evade the ongoing fusillade. The closer targets hadn't attacked him, so he remained high to improve his dive at the ones who had. He screamed in rage when a bullet scraped one of his wings, and Cali's eyes widened in shock. "His scales are magical. They should have protected him."

Tanyith reached the obvious conclusion before she did. "Holy hell. They have anti-magic bullets."

She'd heard of them but had been fairly sure they weren't available in New Orleans. Usually, the expensive and rare ammunition was restricted to the military and the AET forces that some cities had to counter magical threats. "Well, that'll make this more interesting. Let's do it." Before he could try to dissuade her, she launched herself on a trajectory that would take her directly into the ranks of the Zatoras and he followed only a beat later.

Fyre discharged a frost attack at the enemies who'd shot him and they flung themselves aside hastily. The

Atlanteans took advantage of the moment to join the fray and released lightning at their human foes. The humans found cover behind trash cans and elevated stairs to protect them from the first barrage.

Cali landed cleanly and focused on the man in the tan coat since one of the others had referred to him as the boss. He raised the pistol to aim at her, but she had already initiated a quest to reach his mind. She slipped past his mental barriers and made him sneeze as he pulled the trigger, which sent the bullet wide. Before he could aim another, she fired a force blast at his chest that spun him behind a parked car, although he managed to dodge the full strike. Irritated, she surged ahead to get a better angle on him.

A force bolt pounded between her shoulder blades and propelled her forward. She tucked and rolled into a somersault and came out of it on her feet. Not only did the Zatora have his pistol aimed squarely at her, but one of the Atlanteans readied himself for his second assault. Apparently, he thought this might be a good way to remove her from the equation without officially breaking the rules that governed their conflict.

Sure, let him shoot me and you look all innocent. Enemy of my enemy and all that, I guess. Bastards. Now, you've made me mad.

CHAPTER TWO

In quick succession, Cali dispatched a magic force blast at both her enemies before they could act against her. The first knocked the pistol out of the Zatora's hands and his look of shock as it careened away was deeply rewarding. The second failed to connect but drove the Atlantean into hiding. She sent a thought to Fyre to tell him to target the magical gang members and turned toward the man in the tan coat.

He was in mid-twist in an attempt to retrieve his fallen weapon when her bracelets completed their transformation into black Escrima sticks with etched scarlet runes. She hurled them both, the first high and the second low. The shorter distance diminished the impact, but it was still sufficient to trip him very effectively and he landed hard with a grunt. She scanned for the men with the rifles.

One was to her left, the farthest from their original position, and sighted at the closest Atlantean. The other was directly in front of her and his rifle already spat bullets at Tanyith. She gave an involuntary shout of warning. In the same moment, he saw the danger and elevated sharply on a blast of magical force.

The weapon swung upward to aim at him again and her instinct kicked in. Her body lurched into motion toward the assailant, but it was very clear that neither her momentum nor her physical powers would be sufficient to stop him before he shot her partner. In the realm of mental magic, though, time acted differently. She reached out with her mind and found the protective shell around his.

Many magicals trained to build up their resistance, but only the most meditative humans had anything more than the most basic defense. Her foe clearly was not on the path to enlightenment. She darted through one of the plentiful mental gaps and primed him for distraction, then made him imagine a roaring Draksa on his left.

The man flinched, whipped his weapon around, and created holes in the siding of the closely packed buildings that bounded the street. She reached him before he could gain his bearings and positioned herself on the opposite side of him from the Atlanteans. Her first punch landed on his kidney as she darted past and spun to face him. When he arched his back from the pain, an uppercut that carried the full strength of her twisting and rising body struck his chin, lifted him from his feet, and dropped him bonelessly to the cobblestones.

Fyre was only a blur in her peripheral vision in the instant before he powered into her. She dimly heard the gunshots as they tumbled and as she landed beneath him, the realization that he'd saved her swept through her and left the acid taste of disaster narrowly avoided on her tongue. "Get up high, buddy," she muttered quietly. "I'll distract 'em and you freeze 'em."

She rolled into a backward somersault to rise to her feet and summoned her sticks to her hands again in time to block a fire beam from the female Atlantean.

"You're breaking the rules, witch," Cali yelled and raced toward the attacker with her weapons crossed to continue absorbing the magical attack.

The other woman sneered and while she might have been attractive, her face was sweaty and her mascara ran in dark streaks under each eye. Her shiny, long black hair was in a tangle, and her standard-issue Atlantean gang uniform of jeans and a hoodie looked overly worn. "I don't give a damn about the rules. The higher-ups are gonna be happy you're dead no matter how it happens."

Fyre's ice breath washed over her and coated her in an instant. It cut off Cali's opportunity for a reply and she smothered the threat she'd had ready. A quick twist revealed that the man in the tan coat had retrieved his weapon and now attempted to find a clear shot at her. One of the Atlantean men sprawled about halfway between her and the human gang, bleeding from several holes in his chest. Tanyith stood over the still form of the third Zatora, his foot raised over the man's head like he intended to trample him to finish the fight.

"Tanyith, left," she shouted and threw her sticks again. The human gang leader dodged them easily but it gave her partner time to recognize the danger and launch himself toward the rooftops.

Okay, two Zatoras are down but alive, one Atlantean is bleeding, and the other is a popsicle. Where's the third?

The answer came as a blast of lightning from behind a nearby set of stairs. It almost caught her but she'd noticed his hands as they rose into view and summoned a reflexive shield. The force barrier absorbed the energy and channeled it away into nothingness. Before she could launch her own attack, gunfire exploded and he fell. She craned her head upward to locate the source and saw matching glints on rooftops on both sides of the street.

She sensed Fyre heading to one and hoped Tanyith would deal with the other, but it would be too risky to attack the Zatora leader without knowing for sure. With a growl of frustration, she launched herself toward the opposite side of the road from the Draksa. The man on the roof leveled the rifle at her and fired as she landed. The first bullet struck between her feet but she was already moving as the barrel climbed. A clean cartwheel to her left —one of the few gymnastics moves she was comfortable with—carried her mostly out of the path of the incoming rounds. One caught the reinforced heel of the boots she'd taken from her parents' bunker but it failed to penetrate.

Thanks again, guys. She missed them whenever she thought of them, but now that she had accepted the mantle of family matriarch, her feelings had changed. They were no longer entirely painful but were tempered with her responsibility to keep their legacy alive and accomplish the tasks they'd begun. *Starting with protecting my city from scumbags like these.*

Cali threw the two sticks in sequence this time and they tumbled toward her attacker. She didn't have an angle to deliver a force blast without the risk that it might hurl him off the roof, so she muttered a curse and followed them in. He wrenched the barrel down and positioned the weapon in the perfect place to intercept the projectiles she'd hurled and still fire at her. *Damn. He's good. Unfortunately for him, I'm better.*

With less than a second to spare, she created a sheet of force magic over the roof and as he pulled the trigger, she slid like a runner going toward home plate. The virtually frictionless surface channeled her momentum directly into his shins, and the sharp kick she delivered as she arrived knocked them out from under him. A snapping sound signified at least one fracture and he howled in pain as she rose, kicked his rifle off the building, and used her force magic to cushion her leap off the building before she paused and surveyed the battlefield.

Fyre had apparently already dealt with the enemy on his side—or Tanyith had—and the Draksa swooped toward the street. The man in the tan suit fired at him and he broke off his attack run and circled to approach from another direction. The use of a revolver would limit the shots, and the canny dragon lizard forced him to waste bullets. She sent admiration and received a distinct lack of humility in return.

With a shake of her head, she dispatched a precisely aimed force blast to knock the gun out of the Zatora leader's hand again and stood over the weapon before he could recover it. She kicked it back with her heel. "It's a pretty weapon but not the most practical choice."

He scowled. Up close, he was vaguely handsome with a strong, clean-shaven face and the build of a runner, from what she could see of the lines of his body. His tie was plain blue and he'd apparently left his suit jacket at home in favor of the trench coat.

"There are different definitions of practical," he replied. "The jerk over there is still alive after taking three rifle rounds. One shot from me would have put him all the way out, easy."

"Too bad you couldn't hang onto it."

"You'll get yours, waitress," he countered with a shrug. She raised an eyebrow and he laughed. "Of course I know who you are. There's only one redhead teenager who thinks she's cool for mixing it up with her betters."

She glared at him. "First, age is only a number. Second, everyone in the city is better than you and your buddies. So, watch this." She yanked her phone out of her pocket, dialed, and pressed the speaker button at the right moment.

"Barton here. What do you need?" She grinned at the response.

Cali put as much sweetness in her tone as she could manage. "Hey, Detective. A number of gang members seem to have been involved in a fight with each other. You should send one of those things. You know, the cop van."

A heavy sigh from the other end of the line preceded her exasperated reply. "A paddy wagon? Is that what you mean?"

"Yeah, that." Tanyith stepped beside her with a small smile on his face.

"You do realize that term is completely politically incorrect and offensive to the Irish, right?"

"I'm not trying to offend anyone other than you.

Speaking of which, I'm here with your boyfriend and he's all hot and sweaty."

A rueful laugh escaped Detective Kendra Barton. "Tay, is anything she says true?"

He replied cheerfully and completely ignored the gang member. "I am hot, I am sweaty, and there are many injured gang members around. Oh, and a seriously injured one, so send an ambulance too. I gave him a little healing potion but he'll need additional attention."

The Zatora leader across from her shifted like he considered making an attempt to run, and Cali wagged a finger at him. "See you soon, Detective." She punched the button to end the call and stared at the only conscious representative of the human gang. "So you and your buddies attacked the Atlanteans. What's up with that? Is it a change of policy? I thought we were live-and-let-live at the moment."

He shrugged. "It's above my pay grade. I do what I'm told." His gaze cut toward his watch, and Cali realized delaying might not be a good idea in case he had backup on the way.

"Okay. So, here's the deal. You get to go back and tell Grisham he needs to knock it off. With idiots from New Atlantis messing around in our city, he thinks it's a good time to pick another fight? No. Bad plan. He—and you— need to stand the hell down and right now."

The man laughed. "I'm sure he'll be real receptive, waitress."

"Well, you better sell him on it, butthead, or he'll wind up with more trouble than he can bear." Sirens intruded on the edge of her hearing. "You should probably get moving while you're still able to." He made a move toward his pistol where it lay on the ground behind her, and she shook her head. "No, no. That's my souvenir to remember you by. Speaking of which, bye."

He snarled his anger. "I'll get that back, just so you know."

She put her hand over her heart. "I feel threatened. Don't you feel threatened, Tay?"

Tanyith nodded. "I do. Maybe we should end that threat right here."

Cali frowned at the sudden anger that radiated from him. "Now, now. If we do that, our good friend Grisham won't get the message. No, we can let him go this time." She waved dismissively at the Zatora. "Go on. Get. Shuffle off. Hoof it. Scram. Skedaddle. Other clever sayings."

The sirens were probably more responsible for his departure than her urging. She spun to face her ally. "What the hell, man? You don't need to cause any extra trouble, either."

He shook his head. "I guess I'm on edge. I haven't slept all that great since we returned from New Atlantis."

"Maybe you should see a doctor." She jogged toward the ice-encased Atlantean. With a careful application of fire, she melted the ice on the woman's back enough that she could access the backpack. She unzipped it and removed the drugs it held, then stuffed the small packets into her pockets. The sirens were really close now, which was her exit cue.

"Since I don't want to get caught with this on me, I'm out of here. I'll take it to Zeb, and you can talk to him about how much you need to deliver to your new friends in New Atlantis. He can give the rest to the council. I'm sure they can put it to good use—maybe work on a counter-drug or something."

He laughed and some of his familiar mirth returned to his face. "A counter-drug? Do you mean an antidote?"

Cali blew out an annoyed breath. "Whatever. Say hi to your girlfriend for me. Try to keep your hands to yourselves in front of the other police." She launched herself at the rooftop where Fyre awaited her and shook her head at him. "Everyone's a jerk today except you and me, buddy."

He laughed. "Except me, you mean."

She gave him a fake scowl. "Sure, scale-face. Everyone's a critic." She circled her arms in the air and a portal drew itself into being to reveal the basement of the Drunken Dragons Tavern on the far side. "Let's go. I don't want this stuff near me for a second longer than necessary."

CHAPTER THREE

Z eb gazed at the Thursday-night crowd, which was a little larger and a little louder than normal. It filled two-thirds of the three long tables that stretched the length of the common area. Cali navigated the patrons with her usual ease, harassed those who responded best to it, and treated the others with varying degrees of respect. Watching her work the room was always a pleasure, as she had the perfect ability to be whatever the customer needed while not compromising her true self.

His inner monologue had gnawed at him lately, and it surfaced with a snarl. *At least someone here isn't compromising their true self.*

The dwarf shook his head. The decision to retire from adventure and seek a life of contemplation while running the Drunken Dragons was not something he ever seriously regretted—on a conscious level, anyway. His eyes strayed to Valerie, the battle-ax above the bar, with which he'd spent many a year on the road seeking his fortune.

Much of that windfall had been consumed in the usual

ways, but what remained had set him up with this comfortable end to his working days, however long they might last. He sighed and let the worry fade—not resistance, merely acknowledgment of it before he allowed it to flow away. Cali bounced up the three wide stairs to the bar and set empties on its well-preserved wooden surface. She sounded slightly out of breath. "Two ales, four ciders, and an order of stew."

"Get the stew yourself, girl. I'm a bartender, not a chef."

She laughed, the attempt to make him do it an ongoing joke, and retrieved a bowl to fill it from that day's version of the huge cauldron of stew—a blend of lamb, beef, and root vegetables with dark beer for flavor. The pot simmered constantly over a small fire. When she returned, she loaded the beverages he'd pulled onto a tray and offered him a grin. "That was fairly quick. Not bad for an old man."

He shook his head as she departed and stroked his lush black beard and mustache. The few people seated at the bar itself included some of his most regular customers, and he refreshed their drinks without waiting for a request. Their tabs were usually settled eventually, more or less, and he wasn't too worried about a free glass here and there. What was most important was that his guests were happy, comfortable, and most of all, peaceful.

Peace. That's what I need. His internal voice disagreed but he let that slide past him without latching onto it and submerged himself in the routine tasks of bartending for the mostly magical crowd.

At the end of the evening, he watched the patrons flow toward the exit door—Kilomea, wizards, witches, gnomes, elves, and even a couple of the other dwarves who were part of the small contingent of their people in New Orleans. Cali sat across the bar from him after she finished clearing the tables, and he put a soft cider in front of her. Her throat worked as she drained it, and he pulled a second with a smile.

She sighed. "So, how much did Tanyith take?"

Zeb shook his head. "More than half. These people he's working for will be trouble."

The girl nodded. "I know. I'll find a way to get him out from under their thumb before too long." She laughed. "We'll have to. If I keep winning the ritual battles, I'll need his help when we reach the bigger numbers." He felt a pang of guilt and knew he should volunteer to assist her with the fights but at the same time, he was also aware that it wouldn't be a good thing for anyone if he did. The two beliefs coexisted uncomfortably, and he did his best to not allow them any additional purchase in his thoughts or feelings.

"You'll find who you need, I'm sure."

"Do you plan to give the rest to the council?"

He nodded. "As soon as you get yourself out of here, I'll set up."

She yawned. "I could help." Another yawn demanded her full attention and he waited for it to finish.

With a grin, he replied, "I'm good. Thanks for the offer, though. I think maybe you should get to sleep."

Cali nodded. "Fyre had better not be laying on my side of the bed. Damn lazy lizard." She walked away and mumbled under her breath as she headed down the stairs. Portals were only possible in two locations in the tavern—

the basement for friends and the secret chamber off the basement for council members after he released the protective measures blocking them.

Zeb had gone over every inch of the tavern when he'd taken the building over and layered ward upon ward to protect himself and those he served. Now, it was a simple matter to walk the common room and dribble power into them to keep them going each evening. He paid particular attention to those that secured the front door, as they weren't active when the tavern was open and required an extra push to re-engage.

Finally, it was done. The upstairs was clean, the bar was polished with the special solution he used to preserve the Oriceran wood, and the fire under the stew was banked. It was time to head to the lower level for his second gig of the evening. The stairs creaked as he strode down them, and he noted absently that the light bulbs in the basement fixtures needed replacing.

A gesture as he reached the bottom shifted a stack of crates from in front of the false back wall. He pressed his hands into the proper locations on its surface, indistinguishable from the rest, and a broad section moved back and slid off to the right. Another wave released a surge of magic into the lamps in the room to light them and one more sparked the fire in the fireplace, which roared to life.

He nodded with satisfaction. The large round table was clean and polished as always, with seven seats positioned around it. He retrieved a matching number of glasses and set them in place, then spoke the required words to lower the shield that prevented his guests from portaling in. As usual, Malonne was the first to arrive and the Light Elf crossed quickly to avail himself of the casks set beside the door to the basement. The first held red wine, the second Malonne's preferred vintage of white wine, and the third was a seasonal drink of Zeb's own creation, a tart cherry cider.

The other council members appeared at one-minute intervals until all were assembled and seated with drinks beside them. Zeb drew a heavy metal mug of the cider for himself and took his own chair. Today, they'd left him the seat near the council's leader, the wizard Vizidus. The others didn't seem to be in any specific arrangement, which might be because there was no particular issue that brought them together for a change. Tonight was merely a routine meeting.

His inner voice chuckled. *That's how all the best stories start, you know.* Zeb ignored it.

"Thank you all for coming, as always," the white-haired wizard Vizidus intoned. "It is nice to see you without a mammoth octopus or a gang war pressing upon us." The others laughed with varying degrees of mirth. "Our subject tonight is vice in New Orleans."

Delia, the brunette witch with the rock-and-roll style and attitude, rolled her eyes. Today's sweatshirt promoted *My Chemical Romance*, whatever that was. She wore feather earrings that dangled past her shoulders, and there was humor in her expression. "Now that's an expansive topic if ever there was one," she quipped in a raspy tone that was oddly appealing.

Vizidus nodded. "But we're speaking of a specific vice in particular. Well, two. Drugs, both magical and mundane."

Brukirot, the hulking Kilomea who represented the city's largest predators, shook his head. As always, his intelligence came through in his soft voice. "Such things are for the weak."

The witch shrugged. "Or for those who use them ritually. There are witches whose way includes hallucinogens."

He nodded his massive head. "That's a fair comment. But the majority who choose them are weak."

The Light Elf Malonne steepled his long fingers to display his perfect manicure and replied, "Agreed. And unfortunate for those who find themselves trapped by them."

The Dark Elf tapped his long fingers on the table. Invel was one of the dwarf's favorite members of the council and often thought in the same direction he did. It was so on this occasion as well. "But they're here, and that is unlikely to change. The question is, what will we do about it?"

Zeb followed him quickly. "My first inclination is to find another concoction that will help those who are addicted to break the hold it has on them. And also, something we can use to save those who overdose." There were precedents in the human world for both things.

The wizard inclined his head. "Can we all agree that these avenues should be pursued regardless of any other decisions we might make here tonight?" Every person at the table signaled assent, and the mage stroked his beard as he regarded their host. "Are you willing to lead that effort?"

He nodded and Invel added, "I'll help."

Unexpectedly, Delia said the same, and Zeb offered them his thanks. Vizidus took over the conversation again. "So, with that settled, what then of the drugs? Zarcanum is the one made specifically to entice magicals and Shine is the one for the humans. Zeb was able to get a sample of the human one and Invel acquired some of the other. I believe they have been analyzed?"

Scoppic, the gnome who oversaw the arcane library in the city, nodded. Tonight, he wore his work clothes, a light suit with a vest over a cream shirt and tie, as well as a pair of round glasses he'd never worn at a meeting before. "A friend in the police lab did the human one for us and we took the other to Oriceran for an examination. Both are highly addictive and each contains magical substances we don't yet understand."

Malonne sat upright in his chair and appeared shocked. "Wait, both?"

The gnome nodded gravely. "Yes. It is believed that whoever takes the drugs imbibes magic that stays in their system."

Invel frowned. "That sounds like a very bad thing." There were murmurs of assent around the table. "What can we do about that?" he asked. "Really nothing, right?"

Zeb shrugged. "If we could find an antidote of some kind—a way to get rid of it—we could put it in the water or something."

Brukirot laughed, deep and loud. "Perhaps in your ales and offer everyone in town a free glass."

Louder murmurs of assent followed that, and the dwarf shook his head with a smile. "If that's what it takes, you know I'm in."

Vizidus tapped the side of his glass with a fingernail to draw attention to himself once more. "So, then, we are at an impasse. Until we learn more, we cannot work to counteract the drug itself. Scoppic, will you see to continuing the research?" The gnome nodded solemnly, clearly committed to the burden he accepted. "Very well. The question must now be asked—should we act against the Atlantean gang that distributes these drugs?"

The only person to offer anything more than a shrug was the Kilomea. "Yes," he replied. "The easiest way to deal with this threat is to eliminate it at the root. Once that is gone, the issue will wither and die." No swell of agreement rose in response to his statement, and the wizard sighed.

"So again, we collectively choose not to act. My friends, while I do not gainsay your beliefs or your motives, I fear that when we finally decide it is the right time, the real right time will have long passed." Silence greeted his words and lasted for half a minute before he spoke again. "All right, then. Let's plan to meet weekly until this situation has been resolved."

The meeting dissolved into side conversations and goodbyes until the only two left in the room, as usual, were Zeb and Invel. The Dark Elf refilled his glass and limped to the table. He shook his head as he lowered himself gingerly into the seat. "That wasn't all one might have hoped for."

His companion laughed. "No, but it's understandable. They don't see what Cali sees."

"Is what Scoppic told me true? She's one of the Nine?"

"Matriarch of House Leblanc."

"Wow. And you still make her wait tables?"

The dwarf snorted and choked on his drink, then collected himself. "First, that's her choice. Second, she has her head in the right place. And third, hospitality is a noble undertaking."

The Drow grinned. "So you say, my friend. So you say." He sobered, and his expression became grim. "I think things will become much worse here before they get better. And I fear that young Caliste will find the same in New Atlantis."

"I agree. But all we can do is support her—and the city —to the best of our abilities."

"Are we doing that?"

Zeb sighed. "I don't know. I really don't. I think so."

The voice inside him was adamant. *Your best is far more than what you're giving, and you know it.*

That life is behind me. I'll find new ways to be useful. The mocking internal laughter that followed the thought was disconcerting, to say the least.

CHAPTER FOUR

Cali had never been to Pittsburgh, so she arrived a little early for her appointment and used the time to wander downtown. There were far fewer people on the streets than in the French Quarter but probably the same number of sports jerseys. She stood for a while at a distance from the fountain where the rivers met and watched the water reach its apex and fall away for several minutes before she forced her attention away. Thankfully, she'd thrown the black leather coat Nylotte had given her over her jeans and *The Pretty Reckless* t-shirt she wore because the sun did a terrible job of banishing the cold. Her backpack straps rested comfortably over both shoulders.

Now, where the hell is this parking lot? She followed the GPS on her phone and eventually found it directly beside and only slightly above the water level of one of the rivers. In a wall farthest from the boats and the entertainment complex across the way was a gate with arcane symbols around it. She touched the ones she'd been told to and they glowed briefly. As they faded, the barrier did too and permitted her to enter.

She walked down a long paved tunnel that became an equally long rock tunnel. It ended at a great wooden door. When she knocked, a section slid aside to reveal a large eye. "Cali Leblanc, here at Nylotte's invitation."

The peephole slammed closed and the portal creaked open. Beyond it stood a mammoth Kilomea, his scowling face probably sufficient to scare off anyone who wasn't supposed to be there. She wasn't impressed and stared at him in silence.

After half a minute, he spoke in a guttural voice. "You can go in."

Cali nodded her thanks and walked through. Every Kilomea she'd met opened the encounter with the same kind of attitude and lost respect for those who didn't match it. After another substantial trek, the large cavern of the Stonesreach Kemana came fully into view. It was a stunning sight, far larger than she could have imagined an underground city might be. *Underwater, underground...you're really getting around, Cali.* A purple glow emanated from crystals on the roof to illuminate the area below.

A long flight of steps descended to the main part of the city, which appeared to be lined with shops and businesses. At the far end stood a gleaming white palace, and roads ran from it like spikes toward her side of the enormous space. Ridges filled with houses climbed the sides of the bowl. She walked down the stairs as quickly as she could without falling and her legs complained by the time she was halfway down and actively protested at the bottom.

All the magical species she was accustomed to were

present, the rule rather than the exception. Her human looks put her in the minority. Clothing styles and personal grooming varied widely, and she thought a few hours simply watching the unique individuals walking past would be a great way to spend an afternoon.

I don't have time for that now, though. She strode forward down the main thoroughfare, then cut along a small path beside a weapons store. A few minutes later, she emerged on a street that looked and felt darker. The light didn't seem to reach it effectively and the shops somehow appeared more dangerous. She wasn't sure if her magic made her feel that way or merely a natural suspicion, but her speed increased as she walked toward Nylotte's shop.

The door was unlocked when she reached it, and she crossed the threshold with a grateful sigh. The Dark Elf was seated behind a counter to her left and greeted her with a crooked smile. Her long white hair was unbound and fell in a sheet over the shoulders of her dark tunic. "If you weren't such a noble and experienced person, Matriarch of House Leblanc, I'd think it was your first visit to a Kemana."

Cali thought about flipping her off, considered it a second time, then settled for sticking her tongue out at the Drow. "You know it is."

Nylotte chuckled. "Indeed so. Welcome to Stonesreach, Caliste."

She nodded and studied the rest of the room. Behind the elf stood shelves stacked with pots, flasks, and bottles that doubtless contained things arcane. A rack that displayed unfamiliar weapons filled the corner, and a bookshelf covered most of the wall across from the door.

It held the expected tomes but also an abundance of small objects that called to her to touch them. She put her hands in her back pockets and leaned over to peer down the staircase that made up the rest of that side of the room.

When she straightened, it was to find her hostess staring at her with a raised eyebrow. "Are you done?"

Cali laughed. "More or less. I'd love to know what some of those things on the shelves are."

"Oh, I can tell you what they are easily. Too expensive for you." The sense that the other woman wasn't talking only about money came across clearly.

"I'm already in debt to you. You're right, I can't afford more after this trip."

The Drow waved a lazy hand. "Today only costs you a favor in the future."

"That's what I'm worried about."

Nylotte nodded. "Smart girl. So, are you ready to meet him?"

"It was a long journey if I wasn't. Let's do it."

The Dark Elf rose from behind the counter and walked around its edge to give her a small push toward the door. "My contact doesn't do house calls. We'll need to go to his shop."

She followed her out to the street, and the Drow paused to wave at her store. The sensation of wards clicking into place was palpable in the ripple of energy that flowed from her. The woman set off at a notably fast pace, and she hurried to keep up. "What do I owe him?"

"Nothing. I've taken care of that part, which is why you owe me. If it was only an introduction, I would have done it for free." She chuckled. "Well, for less than an open-ended favor, anyway. Those can get you into trouble."

"You're talking about Tanyith, aren't you?"

"Correct on the first guess. Very good." Her demeanor was always snarky and slightly aloof but somehow, the undercurrent of humor also came across quite clearly when she wanted it to. Now was one of those times.

They turned at a cross street near the palace, and she looked at the grand structure. "Who lives there? An Empress?"

"The *lady.*" Her emphasis signaled exasperation.

"I take it you're not a fan?"

Nylotte shrugged and raised a hand toward the next street—the central one her visitor had initially traveled—and they turned. "She's fine. A little conservative for my taste, but not hopeless."

Cali pointed at a shop. "What do they sell?"

"Old books."

She gestured at another. "And there?"

"Poisons."

"Really?" She frowned.

The Dark Elf nodded. "I have no reason to lie to you and several reasons not to since my protege likes you."

"Has Diana been here?" She realized it was a stupid question as the words left her mouth. "Don't answer. Of course she has. You're her teacher. And you don't seem like the kind to make house calls on a regular basis either."

Nylotte laughed. "Well, that's mostly true, although I've found myself in your city far more often than I'd like and for much less profit than I'd like." She stopped and pointed at the shops around as she explained what each was.

"Restaurant, Oriceran food. Restaurant, human food. More books. The fletcher, who has bows and ammunition for them. Even more books. And our destination is there."

Each of the stores had some kind of sign out in front of it, many of them in the same style as the one outside the Drunken Dragons Tavern, painted and hanging from a perpendicular bar. The placard her companion pointed at had a simple image of a golden sword with a red gem at the hilt and a matching stone at the end of the pommel. There was no name on it.

The elf pushed the heavy front door inward and they entered a larger building than Cali expected. She frowned and asked, "Did we portal somewhere else?"

The Drow laughed. "No, but Alessand is clever. He owns several storefronts but from the outside, you wouldn't know it as they look different. They are false fronts carefully crafted to avoid direct notice. That way, he can have his shop here in the corner and his workshop in the other spaces."

Cali peered around the shop portion of the building. Weapons racks covered all the available wall space aside from the front windows and the door at the front and back. Glorious swords of every kind she'd ever seen and many others besides hung in them, gleaming in the light thrown by a chandelier above and lamps set on low tables at the corners. A rectangular island stood in the middle, its surface bare, and looked as if it had been extracted whole from the trunk of a tree. All the furniture was polished wood, and she thought Zeb would be well satisfied with the care the owner took of it "That is clever."

The back door opened and a low voice filled with

humor emerged from the space beyond it. "I do my best." She turned to watch the man—or elf, rather—enter. He wore a tunic that reached from a high collar to below his knees, with black pants visible below and at the slit side as he stepped inside the room. His long brown hair was pulled away from his face; and a heavy-looking ponytail was momentarily evident as he walked. He seemed stronger and bulkier than most of the elves she'd seen before but still had the elegantly pointed ears and the seemingly universal sculpted cheekbones that invoked jealousy every single time she encountered them.

He smiled and crossed to Nylotte to gather her into a hug. The sight was somehow shocking as she'd never pictured the Drow lowering her defenses enough to be touched, much less return the gesture. They both wore smiles when they drew apart.

Well, well, well. Love flourishes everywhere. At this rate, Zeb will be dating soon. She wished for a moment that she'd been able to bring Fyre so he could laugh at her mental jokes but the invitation hadn't specifically included him, and she'd feared making a misstep. *Next time.*

The elf turned his grin to her. "So, you're Caliste Leblanc. Welcome to my shop, Matriarch."

"Cali, please. Just Cali." She shook her head. "Your talent is amazing."

"I have spent a very long time working to make it so." His neutral, matter-of-fact tone suggested he was pleased with the compliment but not arrogant about his abilities. "Have you brought it?"

She nodded and slipped out of the backpack. It made a metallic clank as she set it on the wooden island, and she unzipped it carefully and withdrew the item within. The silver blade gleamed in the room's light, the etchings barely deep enough to cast their own tiny shadows.

Alessand didn't touch the shard and only circled it slowly to examine it from all angles. He crouched to look at the edge, then rose again and grinned at Nylotte. "Now I see why you wouldn't give me a hint."

She laughed almost flirtatiously. "Of course not. Surely a person of your immense talent would want the full challenge. Although letting you know of Caliste's ancestry was a small step along the path."

He nodded. "The family sword of House Leblanc, I presume. One of the nine magical blades bestowed upon the nobility to celebrate the creation of Atlantis."

"New Atlantis?" Cali asked.

"No. The original." He reached out and stroked the weapon gently with a fingertip. "There are rumors of every kind about what they are capable of. What happened to this one?"

She shrugged. "I don't know. When my parents had it, the sword was whole. When it came to me, it...wasn't."

The elf shook his head and looked thoughtful. "I'll be right back." He strode out through the door he'd used to enter.

She turned to Nylotte. "So, you didn't mention that he was cute."

The Drow offered her a pleased smile. "He is finely made, that one. Much like his weapons."

Cali walked closer to the side wall to examine the blades mounted there. The tallest would clearly require a large person using both hands to wield it. She couldn't even imagine carrying it, much less handling it effectively.

Alessand peered at a book when he entered again and turned the pages rapidly, obviously looking for something. He muttered, "Got you," and placed it on the island before he rotated the tome so they could both see it. Spread across both open pages were a series of mostly identical swords. They had long hilts and shining silver-white blades in common, with matching engraved runes. Each pommel was adorned with a different colored gem. He proclaimed, "The Nine Noble Swords of the Nine Noble Houses of Atlantis, where apparently, being noble really matters."

The girl laughed. "Right? They're crazy about it. The whole structure of New Atlantis reinforces how special the Nine are, second only to the monarch."

"It must have taken something significant to shatter your sword. They are truly magical blades—artifacts, really —and frightfully difficult to break with anything other than another magical artifact." He handed the book to Nylotte, who accepted it without protest and gestured for Cali to remove her backpack. She complied as he pulled a large sheet of paper over the island, apparently from a roll hidden in the base. He lifted the metal fragment gingerly, then set it on top of the white material.

He stared at it in silence for almost a full minute. Finally, with a nod, he produced a thick pencil and went to work. He started by outlining the outer edge of the piece she'd brought, then extrapolated from there to sketch the dimensions of the blade as it would have looked whole. Occasionally, he turned to the book for reference. In ten minutes, it was done. He had judged where the likely breaks had occurred based on the imperfections in her fragment and drawn cracks where they would be.

She sighed. His drawing showed five pieces that she didn't have, not counting the pommel. They differed in size and shape but she had to give him credit. "That's impressive work. How sure are you about the breaks?"

Alessand smiled and gave a small shrug. "Somewhere between fairly sure and very sure. You can see on your fragment where the notches are that suggest breakpoints, and I've made some informed guesses based on them. You don't have any other fragments?"

She snorted. "I wish. I think I know where some might be." *Rion damn Grisham the artifact buyer.* "And possibly another." *If the Atlantean shard is part of this, which is far from guaranteed.* "But beyond that, I have nothing."

He nodded. "Bring them, and I'll take a look at them. Perhaps I will see something in them that you've missed." He looked at Nylotte. "And you? Are you going to help her?"

The Dark Elf closed the book and handed it to him. "I already have. I introduced the two of you. What more do you want from me?"

He laughed. "You are working multiple angles, as always." He turned to face Cali. "She knows it is my true passion to work on magical weapons. The ones you see here are all mundane and provide good practice. But if you can find the pieces, it would be my distinct pleasure to rejoin them for you." He looked at Nylotte. "Which means you'd be doing me a favor if you helped her locate them."

The sparkle in the Drow's eyes was unmistakable. "Well then," she all but purred. "How could I refuse?"

CHAPTER FIVE

Rion Grisham had passed a pleasant evening with the newest of his many female companions, dining and drinking at one of New Orleans' most exclusive restaurants. She was upstairs in the hotel room waiting for him, and he was not at all pleased that he sat at the Sheraton bar waiting for the Zatora's mage to arrive. The dim lighting and muffled conversation from the surrounding tables fit his irritated mood perfectly.

At first, he had truly enjoyed having the magical on his team and reveled in the fact that he had discovered a way to counter the biggest dangers from the nonhumans that increasingly filled his city. After several months of the man's borderline insubordination, that had faded. Now, after more than a year and a half as purported allies, Ozahl grated on him. Daily, without a doubt, and on most days, multiple times. He currently looked for a replacement but had begun to learn that there weren't many who were willing to work against their own side. Plus, his inquiries were necessarily minimal as he couldn't allow word to reach the mage that he was trying to replace him.

So now, he nursed his Manhattan and scowled at the entrance with each minute that passed without his subordinate crossing the threshold.

He said this was urgent, so where the hell is he?

As if the thought was a spell, Ozahl appeared and sauntered into the room like he hadn't a care in the world. The mage was dressed strangely out of character in jeans and a fashionable button-down shirt with a subtle gray-on-black pattern that showed when the light caught it at a certain angle. It took him a moment to realize that his instincts were tweaked by the man's hair, which was a far lighter shade of brown than usual, including the eyebrows.

The Zatora shook his head with a frown. "It's about time you got here. I thought you said it was urgent."

The newcomer slid into the tall chair beside him and pointed at the bartender to order a round of the same for each of them. Tension showed in the lines near his eyes. "One of the teams that targeted the Atlanteans was hit tonight. The scumbags laid a trap and your people walked right into it."

Grisham's fist tightened around his glass, and he considered hurling it into the large mirror that made up the back of the serving area above and behind the rows of liquor bottles. "Did we lose anyone vital?"

Ozahl shook his head. "No. Middle-level only. No one important."

He had a different view of the importance of every member of his organization than the mage did, but there was no point in arguing about it now. "So why is it urgent?"

"They left a message for us. Well, for you." He paused as the bartender delivered the drinks, his black vest, white shirt, and bow tie a reminder that they were in a public place and he needed to control his temper.

Once again wishing he was anywhere but there, he growled under his breath and settled his features into a calm mask. "And this message said?"

The mage took a sip of his drink before he replied. "You're next, Rion. That's what it said."

The gang leader emptied his glass to the ice cubes in a long swallow. "Did you bring it? So we can have it analyzed?"

His companion laughed darkly. "It was written in blood on a nearby building. I incinerated it as soon as I arrived so no one else would see it and think you were vulnerable."

"That was a good decision." His mind sifted through possible responses while his body signaled for a third drink. Both a plan and the glass appeared simultaneously. "So, they believe they'll slow us by threatening me, do they? Well, they're about to discover how wrong they are. For now, maintain the status quo but warn our people to be extra careful about traps. If there's any worry, fade. But since they can't cover everyone, we'll still steal the drugs from them where we can."

Ozahl nodded. "Will do. And after that?"

"I'll let you know." Grisham beckoned for the bartender. "Put the drinks on my room tab. My friend here can have whatever he wants." He stood and patted his companion awkwardly on the shoulder. "Good work, as always. Now, I have someone waiting for me—assuming she hasn't fallen asleep."

Ozahl watched his supposed boss walk unsteadily from the bar. The man's expensive suit looked a little tight.

He's been hitting the bottle far more lately, looks like. He smiled and ordered drinks for a nearby table on Grisham's tab, then left his own mostly unfinished and headed to the door.

Canal street was busy, as usual, with cars and people going in every direction, even into the final hours of Friday night. Past experience told him they'd still be at it into the early hours of Saturday morning as well. Once upon a time, he'd been a member of a group that partied the night away after they'd perpetrated mildly nefarious deeds, but that was many years before. He craved a quieter existence now, filled with frequently major nefarious deeds that inched him closer to the life of power and privilege he'd always coveted.

Speaking of craving... He pictured Danna as he'd last seen her, stretched out in bed sleeping, and hoped that her alleged superior wouldn't keep her working for the whole night. Their time together was less plentiful than either of them liked as they furthered their individual plans to seize the resources of the New Orleans gangs and use them to push for primacy in New Atlantis. When one of the noble houses fell, they would need treasure, strength, and audacity in equal measures to step into the void.

And it was time to take another big stride in that direction. The first alley he checked had two people making a deal of some kind in it, but the next was empty. He hurried out of sight of the main street, summoned a portal, and stepped through onto a rooftop that overlooked one of the Atlanteans' primary drug distribution locations. A little smaller than where he, Lila, and Dalton had struck before, this position had the advantage of being at the intersection of two less-traveled streets. Here, they worked the corners with the seller on one, the money person on the next, and the individual holding the drugs on a third.

Tonight, he identified an additional member of the magical contingent, a hard-looking man who stood idly on the fourth corner and attempted to look like a junkie. His eyes were far too alert to achieve that particular illusion, though. Ozahl decided that might make the attack the Zatora hit team had planned a little more challenging than usual.

The humans had brought only three, one woman and two men. They wore the jeans and button-down shirt combination that was the uniform of the lowest level of the organization, and he laughed at the fact that the woman's look was very similar to his own.

Better her than the gruesome twosome following her, though. He knew all of them and they had about a brain and a half if you added it all together, most of it lodged in her skull.

This ought to be good. He watched as they reached the point where they had an angle on two of the Atlanteans. The supposed junkie was on the opposite side of a wide utility pole from their approach, and the one who held the product was protected by stone walls that ran up both sides of the stairs he sat on and blocked him from their view and them from his.

The Zatoras drew suppressed pistols from under the backs of their shirts and pulled the triggers without preamble. Two aimed at the figure across the street on the right and the third at the Atlantean nearest them on the right. One of the longer shots missed and the bullet drove into the brick side of a building with a loud thwack, but the other caught the target in the shoulder. The woman's shot at the closest enemy struck the center of his back and he fell face-first.

The gang member's melodic voice was a counterpoint to her harsh words. "You two look for the third. I'll make sure the loser over there is dead." His bird's-eye view of the situation allowed him to watch the man with the backpack full of drugs draw his pistol at the sound of the gunshots and crouch in readiness behind the short wall. He locked gazes with the fourth member and nodded, and they moved as one.

Both men rushed from hiding with their weapons raised. The Atlantean shot the incoming Zatora with a triple burst, then spun to race away. The other fired at the woman, who turned calmly and returned her own barrage when his rounds went wide and the assault hurled him from his feet. She surged forward and stopped in the middle of the street and the car that had entered the area during the battle stopped behind her with a squeal of tires. She continued to pull the trigger until the gun clicked empty but the volley felled the runner. The driver turned the vehicle frantically around the corner and accelerated to clear the scene.

She advanced calmly to her fallen foe and retrieved the backpack, then joined her ally at the side of their wounded teammate. The heads shook in unison and told the story.

One of theirs gone, all the Atlanteans dead or dying. Good job, Zatoras. Too bad you won't have the chance to celebrate your success.

Ozahl launched himself off the roof and used force magic to cushion his landing behind the two gang members. They turned and broke into smiles at the sight of him. The woman was about to speak when he delivered a magical shadow bolt into her chest. The attack catapulted the Zatora onto her back, and her skull struck the pavement with a loud crack. The man beside her lost precious seconds to shock but managed to draw his gun before the wash of fire swept over him. He screamed and thrashed in an effort to extinguish the flames but his shrieks cut off in moments when he died. The mage sighed at what he considered the ineptitude of the humans.

The gun had fallen from the woman's hands and she lay on her back, panting, and her eyes were defocused. Blood pooled around her head. *Perfect. So convenient.* He knelt beside her and used a thin line of flame to cut a section of her shirt away, then dropped it in the dark-red liquid.

She whispered, "Why?"

He shrugged. "For the same reason you did what you did to the Atlanteans. There's something I want and this is the path to get it. I'd say I'm sorry you wound up in the middle, but that would be a lie." She seemed like she was about to reply, perhaps to challenge him or beg for mercy, when her eyes fluttered closed and she lost consciousness. He waited and watched until her breathing stopped, then ensured that all the fallen were beyond being able to tell the truth of what had occurred.

With the bloody rag, he wrote, "You're next, Rion," on the closest wall. He incinerated the fabric when he was done and checked himself carefully for bloodstains. Satisfied that there were none, he sent Grisham another text for an urgent meeting first thing in the morning.

I hope it ruins your night, you giant bag of ooze. With a smile at the mental image of the man's rage, Ozahl portaled home to await his partner.

CHAPTER SIX

Usha, comfortably seated in her preferred place at the far end of the long bar that ran along the main room of the club, waited patiently and watched as the last stragglers departed the Shark Nightclub. She and her second in command, Danna Cudon, had spent the evening enjoying the music, laughing at the people, and discussing in the broadest of terms the potential plans for expanding the nightclub or opening another location.

With the influx of business generated by the demand for the gang's new drugs, Zarcanum and Shine, a corresponding need to increase their ability to launder the money gained from it had emerged. They weren't experts at such things, and the gang leader intended to seek guidance from Empress Shenni and her advisors, but it had been an enjoyable discussion if not entirely practical. There was no one in the world, save the Empress herself, who she felt more comfortable with—more able to be her true self with—than Danna.

Tonight, the woman was dressed in a navy business suit

with a purple shirt and crimson tie that somehow all worked perfectly together. She'd taken to wearing more fashionable footwear of late, and the red pumps were a perfect match to the shade at her neck. Given the workload placed on her, it was a wonder she had time to shop.

Maybe she has a boyfriend or girlfriend taking care of that for her. It might be worth putting someone on her to find out so I can tease her about it.

Finally, the door was closed and locked, and the work lights came on overhead. She nodded and finished her drink, then stood and stretched. "Let's head to the back." Danna rose and followed her down the hallway to the office, where they each took one of the couches. The suited woman sat carefully on the edge of the seat, and Usha smoothed her long dress as she reclined at full length on the cushions and stared at the ceiling above, a throw pillow under her head and her feet on the far arm of the furniture.

"So, talk to me about the protection you've introduced against the Zatoras." The attempted attack a few nights before that Caliste had foiled had alerted them that the criminal organization now actively targeted their people. They'd discussed options for retaliation but hadn't put any into motion yet and both agreed that the topic still needed further conversation before actions were taken.

Danna sighed. "They have the strategic advantage since we need to be more or less in the same locations in order to reach our clients. For now, they haven't been able to strike the Zarcanum because we continue to take care of those people personally. It's proving to be a real strain, however."

The Atlantean leader nodded. Her second had asked for

more person-power to support their expansion and so far, none had materialized. The risk of bringing someone in who might act against them was high but soon, there would be no other choice. "Well, that's something anyway. And the Shine?"

"It's a completely different story. They know where we'll be and they appear more often than not. Our people will run and regroup if they see anyone and each team now has an additional member in support. The situation is cutting into the profits, but not so much that it's a huge issue—yet."

The implication that it would become one was obvious and again, without more personnel, addressing it would be a challenge. "What do you recommend?"

Danna shrugged. "We should launch retaliatory strikes —hard. Wipe them out so they can't rise up again."

She closed her eyes and considered the idea in silence. It wasn't the first time that solution had been suggested and it held definite appeal. With the Zatora organization shattered, there wouldn't be much in the way of opposition, at least until someone stepped in to fill the void. Her Atlanteans would be able to expand rapidly and claim a large portion of what the humans currently possessed.

And yet, that would require more people too. I'll have to quit whining and ask the Empress.

Usha hated the idea of imposing on her ruler, especially after the monarch had provided enforcers for the battles against Caliste Leblanc. If that had delivered better results, it would have been easier to request more support, but the damned girl had proven to be both skilled and resilient and was an ongoing challenge.

Her sigh was both regretful and impatient. "No, we can't do it. Not yet. We don't have the people to succeed, not even if we managed to gain complete surprise."

"What if we could get most of them into one place?"

The gang leader turned her head to gaze at her subordinate. "Come again?"

Danna responded with a thin smile. "What if we arranged things so the whole gang was drawn together for some reason? We could assault that location with everything we have and boom, game over for the Zatora organization."

"That's an interesting possibility. What would make them gather like that?"

"A funeral." The words were flat but urgent. Clearly, her second had thought this approach through and liked it.

She nodded slowly. "It would have to be someone high up."

"Grisham has three lieutenants, according to our watchers, at least one of whom we've seen in person at the Tavern. One is remarkably like him, the second could pass as muscle but is evidently more, and the third must be a magical, or so they say."

Usha sat and leaned her back against the cushions to face Danna without looking at her. "What kind?"

"Not a Kilomea, anyway." She laughed. "He's humanoid with no sign of pointed ears, so I would guess a wizard."

"How did Grisham get a magical to work for him?"

The woman merely shrugged again. "Who knows? Money, probably. Everyone needs money."

"Was he one of the two at the bar?" She frowned as she thought back.

Her subordinate shook her head. "I don't think so. The first one was there, though."

"Okay. I guess this requires more information. So, do what you can to find out what we need and we'll see where things go." Danna nodded. "Now, we must work on the Leblanc challenge. The Empress's desire to turn her to our side makes the situation significantly more complicated so it would be best if we could simply kill her during one of the ritual battles."

"We're ready for the next one, the four-on-four. I've brought in a couple of experts from out of town."

Usha smiled. "Excellent. But just in case, let's get to work on the backup plan to weaken her support system. There are several people who we know are important to her. The convict, Tanyith." She would have started with him on general principles, as he had been an irritant since the instant she'd first laid eyes on him before he'd been sent to Trevilsom prison. However, that wasn't practical, and cool-headed rationality was what the moment required. "The dwarf who owns the bar. The kid she performs with. And the relative."

The other woman nodded. "If we cast a little wider, she's been seen going into the library fairly often lately. The gnomes are most likely a connection. And, of course, her Aikido teacher. And the Draksa." The last word came out as a snarl.

"Certainly, the creature would provide the greatest loss, but it would be difficult to separate him from her. Plus, he's formidable in his own right. The dwarf, too, would be devastating. But I think there's more readily plucked fruit available that would have an outsized impact."

"The boy."

Usha smiled. "You know my thinking so well. Yes, the one she spends time with in Jackson Square. He would be an easy target as long as she wasn't with him. It would also send a clear message that those around her are in danger because of her and that they are generally unable to protect themselves from us. Finally, it avoids getting into the level of a blood feud that harming a relative would."

Danna raised an eyebrow with a smirk. "We're already at that level."

She chuckled. "True, true, but the girl doesn't know it was us who sent her parents on to the next life. And there's no need for her to, not for a while anyway—if ever. No, I think the choice is clear."

"When?"

"I can't see a reason to wait. As soon as you can do it safely. See to it personally."

Her second rose with a nod. "Excellent. I'll get started on it in the morning."

Usha grinned. "Do you have a hot date?"

"Not tonight." The woman rolled her eyes. "It's far too late for that. No, I need to get my beauty sleep. This"—she gestured to indicate herself—"doesn't happen by itself."

They laughed together, and the woman exited and closed the door softly behind her. Usha lay on the couch again and decided she was too tired to bother to portal home when the furniture she was already on was so comfortable.

Danna stepped out onto the nighttime street and decided she needed a short walk to clear her head from the drinks and the smoke and the many potential actions running amok in her mind. Keeping the overarching plans she shared with her true partner out of her thoughts while dealing with Usha was a challenge.

Much like Caliste Leblanc and the Empress herself.

There was still time enough for her to get home and spend a few hours with the mage before sleep would claim them both if nothing had changed since they'd last seen one another. She looked forward to the day when they would leave their double lives behind and take their rightful places among the New Atlantean elite.

She prayed for a way to accomplish it without destroying Usha in the process. In truth, the other woman was as close as she'd ever had to a true friend, aside from the mage. They'd discussed bringing her in with them on the plan, but it was too risky. If word got out, their long game might be undermined. She hoped to invite her to join them—not as part of their household but on their property as her most trusted advisor and confidant. It was perhaps a step down for the woman and she could only pray her pride would allow her to accept it. Of course, the chances were better if the Empress fell at another's hand, which would leave Usha disconnected from her own support system.

Exactly like we'll do with you, Cali. I hope you have a performance planned with your friend for this afternoon because it'll be the last one you'll ever have.

CHAPTER SEVEN

Cali sighed in exasperation as she peered at the Light Elf seated at the back of the Tavern. "Look, it's simple. If you like Guinness and you like cider, you'll like a snakebite. If you dislike either of those, I would highly recommend you don't order one."

The patron shook his head thoughtfully and his perfectly styled long blond hair swayed in a way he no doubt thought enticing. She risked a glance at his date and the female Light Elf rolled her eyes and proclaimed, "Well, I'll try it."

"Wonderful." She managed to unclench her teeth enough to speak coherently. "Would you like to make it two?" His reply was preempted by the loud thud when the front door slammed against the wall. Every eye turned to the entrance as one of her best friends staggered through, his chest heaving and his eyes wild. She rushed over to him and pulled him to a chair at the bar. "Dasante, what's wrong?"

Zeb pushed a soft cider into his hand, and he drank deeply. Sweat stood out on his dark skin and his wavy black hair was in disarray. His magician's costume of black jeans and button-down shirt wasn't a great choice for running, clearly. Finally, he coughed, expelled a lungful of air, and seemed to draw in the ability to speak with the next inhale.

"There was an attack...in Jackson Square. A busker was found dead in the bushes. He—" Dasante took another long drink before he finished the thought. "He looked very similar to me and he was close to my usual position. I worked with Jen and Jax on the other corner, closer to Cafe du Monde. I didn't see what happened but heard the screaming and went to see what happened. Then, I guess I panicked." He shook his head. "I don't remember anything between seeing the body and opening the door here."

He rose on shaky legs. "I have to get back and make sure they're okay."

Cali presumed he meant the other two buskers, but he might have referred to everyone in the square. His heart was at least three sizes too big. She pushed him into the chair. "No, you stay right here until you can function again and Zeb will call a ride to take you home." The dwarf nodded and his expression signaled approval as well as agreement.

She tossed her notepad and pen on the bar. "I, on the other hand, will go to find out who did this so I can kick their asses into the bloody ocean."

Where, hopefully, they'll be eaten by a shark. Slowly.

Side streets and rooftops provided the best route for Cali to be able to use her magic to amplify her speed without attracting notice. Letting some of the constant pressure trickle out was a good feeling and one she could get used to.

Exactly what Emalia warned me about. But if this doesn't call for it, I'm not sure what would.

Fyre flew overhead and kept watch for potential ambushes since her reaction to the news would have been fairly easy to predict.

She was positive that whatever had happened had something to do with her, at best, and was her fault, at worst. She no longer believed in coincidence, not when so many different people and groups took an active interest in her life. No, this was an attack, albeit indirectly. It was a small step from there to conclude that Dasante had been the intended target and only luck or stupidity had intervened to save him from being the one found in the bushes.

When she reached the alley before the building that bordered the square, she paused to collect herself. Once her breathing had slowed sufficiently, she leapt from the three-story roof and used force magic to cushion her landing. She strode to the end of the narrow street, turned right on Decatur, and walked briskly toward the position she and Dasante usually called home. Fyre flew lazy circles above and sent a steady thread of assurance across the mental channel that connected them.

Flashing lights illuminated the darkness in red and blue, and bright yellow caution tape blocked the entrance to the square. She caught a break when familiar features appeared briefly in the beam of a swung flashlight. She cupped her hands around her mouth and yelled, "Detective Barton."

The NOPD officer's head spun toward her and revealed the neutral-cop face she had seen the other woman wear a number of times before. "Let her in," Barton called.

The uniformed man who manned the tape lifted it for her with a muttered, "Don't step on any evidence, okay?"

She didn't waste the time to give him the snarky reply the comment deserved. *I'm not an idiot. Even if I weren't studying the field, I've seen at least a couple of episodes of every one of the CSI shows.* She moved carefully through the markers that were seemingly placed at random around the area and arrived at Barton's side. "How bad is it?"

The other woman shrugged. "Murders are always bad but it's worse when it's someone this young who isn't playing the game." She'd explained that term once during a late-night chat at the Drunken Dragons. It was commonly used by gang task forces to refer to those who battled for territory and influence.

"Can I take a look at him?" The detective didn't ask how she knew the victim was male and merely led her to a position where she wouldn't interfere but could see. He was utterly and unnaturally still, the dark skin at his neck stained red by a slash across it that had opened an artery. "Blood loss?" she asked.

Barton nodded. "Most likely. We won't know for sure until the coroner is finished with her examination, but it seems clear." There was always the possibility that the obvious wound had been inflicted to disguise some other cause of death, but that was surely not a possibility in this case.

"Do you have any idea why?"

Her companion stared into her eyes before she responded. "It's too early to tell. Maybe you have something you want to share?"

Cali sighed. "He looks like Dasante. And I have a long list of enemies these days." At the other woman's gesture, she followed her to a less populated part of the square.

The detective stopped and looked at the sky. "Wasn't all that stuff supposed to be kept within a fairly specific set of rules?"

She nodded. "'Supposed to be' seems like the right phrase. Although, as far as I know, the restrictions are only against attacking me, not those I care about."

"So, anyone who knows you is in danger is what you're saying."

The harsh statement made her flinch but her companion wasn't wrong. "Yeah, I guess so."

Barton shook her head but didn't look away. "If we discover evidence connecting this to you, I could attempt to have resources assigned to watch over some of your key supporters. I don't think it will be easy to find, unfortunately. Plus, there's no way to tell which of your many admirers did this as far as I can see."

"Let me try something." She sat cross-legged on the night-chilled pavement. The way her magic had revealed secrets for her like the entrance to her parents' bunker and at the house in New Atlantis had made her wonder if it could do more of that. Now seemed as good a time as any to experiment, given the lack of any other clues.

Ignoring everything around her, Cali focused inward and first stored the cacophony of thoughts that jostled around in her brain. Once they were packed into their corners, she opened a small funnel to allow her power to flow out of her and asked it to find any hints of what had really happened. Previously, it had been able to sense other magics, and it was her hope that if magic had been involved in this killing, there would be some kind of residue she could detect.

Behind her closed eyes, an image of the square formed in outlines like gray strokes on a black background. She turned her head slowly and the picture shifted until she looked at the corner where the body lay in lifeless repose. The lines that outlined it glowed slightly and the slash across the neck shone brighter than the rest. She narrowed her concentration onto that line in an attempt to discern what her magic tried to tell her. A chill ran across her throat along the same vector as his wound, and she was suddenly positive he'd been killed by a shard of magical ice.

Her excitement threatened her focus, so she paused to gather her attention again until it was as thin and precise as a laser beam. A slight glimmer in the air above the body formed into a line as she probed it and connected to a splotch on the iron fence and a place on the roof of the cathedral at the opposite end. Her face twisted in confusion for a moment because the line didn't make sense with the mark on his neck.

Unless there was something that made him look up. A distraction, maybe, like I can do with my mental magic. Yeah, that must have been it.

She stood and brushed her jeans off, then met Barton's expectant eyes. "It was magical, it was ice, and it came from the top of the cathedral."

They both turned to peer at the structure at the far end of the square. "Why ice?" the detective asked. "Is that a clue?"

Cali nodded. "I assume it is. It wouldn't mean anything to someone who didn't know Fyre's magic is ice, but I think that's why they chose it."

"So who knows that?"

She laughed. "The Atlanteans here. The Malniets we fought when they came into the city. Anyone who saw the battle at the docks."

A small rueful smile creased the other woman's face. "So that's not particularly useful then."

"No, not so much." She shook her head. "But hopefully, I'll be able to find something up there."

A frown replaced the smile. "I suppose it makes sense for you to take the first look. But if there's any actual physical evidence, do your best not to ruin it, okay? My people will climb up and work the scene once you're done."

"I would never try to get in the way of you doing your job, Detective." She grinned when Barton rolled her eyes, then jogged away before the woman could find a response.

The small lane to the right side of St. Louis Cathedral, called Pere Antoine alley, provided enough cover for her to launch up to the sloped roof that crowned the structure. From there, she climbed the large decorative block at the front center of the building. As soon as she reached the top of it, she knew she'd found the place where the attack originated. The sightline through the trees was perfect. All that would have been required was a way to get him in there, and the options would have been plentiful if they'd managed to penetrate his mental barriers.

Sadly, there was no actual evidence, physical or magical, to confirm who it was. She clambered to the roof and sat beside Fyre once he landed on the small flat piece that ran along the centerline of the Cathedral. "Did you see anything that might tell us who it was?"

The Draksa shook his head. "No. Not even watchers. Apparently, it wasn't meant as a trap, only as a way to hurt you."

She sighed. "They can't beat me fairly so they go after people I care about. This changes things. It changes things completely."

He nodded. "No more letting enemies walk away from fights, then." It was a statement, not a question, and held overtones of regret.

"Right. No more Miss Nice Matriarch." Cali shook her head. "Let's head down and ask Barton to keep an eye on Emalia, anyway, and Dasante. Everyone else can probably take care of themselves."

Fyre chuckled. "I doubt your great aunt would enjoy hearing you suggest she can't defend herself."

She grinned. "Oh, I know she's up to it. But I need her to help me find out where the rest of the damn sword pieces are so I don't want her distracted." The mirth faded quickly. She wasn't looking forward to what she'd have to do, but her enemies had left her no other choice.

The best thing I can do is get this all over as fast as possible.

Suddenly, the Draksa stiffened. "Do you smell that?"

Cali shook her head and bolted to her feet. "No, what is it?"

He growled, "Fire," and launched skyward. When she saw he was flying on a trajectory to Emalia's shop, she used a force blast to hurtle after him.

CHAPTER EIGHT

As she soared over the trees and the fence that separated the Square from the pathways and streets that bounded it, the first wafts of smoke became visible. The third-floor windows of the long building that bordered the southwest of the area were protected by ornamental shutters, but thin gray vapors drifted out of several of them, including those over Emalia's shop.

Cali landed a dozen feet away from her great aunt's doorway and paused long enough to fling a double blast of force magic into the shutters that covered the second-floor windows. As they splintered and the glass behind them shattered inward, she hoped the woman wasn't hurt by the shards.

Cuts are better than dying. She sent Fyre a telepathic message to tell him to ice the flames inside while she aimed another burst of power at the front door of the fortune teller shop.

She barreled through the opening at a run and yelled for the most important woman in her life. A crash sounded from the back and she slid to a stop as a Draksa slithered into the room from that direction. She thought it was Fyre for an instant—long enough for the creature to belch a wave of fire at her. With a muttered curse, she dove to the left and rolled, and while she impacted with the wall, she at least avoided being cooked.

She darted to her feet and created a force shield that protected her from feet to head and wrapped halfway on either side. It intercepted the next blast, and she stalked forward against the physical pressure of the flames. The walls and ceiling were burning, and the creaking from above was alarming. She ordered Fyre to abandon the attempt to put the fire out and try to reach the stairs to the room in the rear.

Maybe we can surround the beast and kill it, although there might not be enough time.

Sweat coursed down her face and the back of her shirt, and she slapped her head with her free hand when the smell of burning hair reached her nostrils. The dragon lizard paused, maybe to inhale, and she had the sense that if she didn't take decisive action in that instant, she wouldn't have another chance. She knew her force blasts weren't likely to deliver an instant kill, and her fire magic would be useless.

Okay, then, so be it. She sent a second message to Fyre to tell him to get down the stairs right away or fly out immediately and broke into a run.

The enemy Draksa began to breathe flames again as she reached him, but she was already moving out of the path. She thrust the force shield into its face and used it as a sled, vaulted onto it, and slid down the dragon lizard's spine and tail. Before her foe could react, she slid into the back room, where Emalia peered over the small table they'd sat at so often. This now lay on its side in the corner to provide the woman the tiniest measure of cover.

Cali pushed up, flung herself toward the table, and twisted and shouted as she blasted the support beam that ran along the division between the front room and the back with all the force magic she could muster. It cracked, and the weakened structure around it fell. She and Emalia both shouted the commands to summon overlapping shields.

The end of the building collapsed onto them with a thunderous roar. She felt Fyre's panic and sent him soothing feelings and the message that she and her great aunt were okay. His emotions calmed but still held simmering anger.

Inside their bubbles, Emalia uttered a choked laugh. "You never were subtle, Caliste."

She shook her head helplessly and laughed for a solid minute before she regained control of herself, wiped her eyes, and wrapped the older woman in a hug. "I'm so glad you're safe. How did you fight the Draksa off?"

She shrugged. "It threw flames so I blocked with ice. I knew it was temporary since the building caught fire, but I didn't see another option. I merely hoped to hold out until someone rescued me. When I tried to portal out, the spell wouldn't finish."

"They planned this well. Two attacks and the second one timed to try to get me, too. They'd certainly have thought of having an ally nearby to make sure there wasn't an easy escape."

"So, what now? We can't stay in the bubble forever."

"We'll try to portal again in a short while. Eventually, they'll assume we're dead and go away. Until then, let's talk about finding the other sword pieces."

It took almost two full hours before whoever was blocking their ability to portal departed, either because they assumed they were dead or simply because they gave up. Cali led her great aunt through a portal to the Dragons, told Fyre they were safe and he should fly home to watch over Dasante, and was surprised to find Zeb still behind the bar when they climbed the stairs.

"I assumed you'd wind up here," he said. "Besides, there were things I needed to do."

She nodded and escorted her great aunt to one of the chairs, then sat beside her. Zeb handed them both ciders, bowls of stew, and what was left of that day's bread. They ate in silence for several minutes before something occurred to her. "What do you do with the leftover bread? It's never here the next day."

The dwarf laughed. "I give it to the birds, the ducks, or the squirrels. Whatever I find first."

Emalia smiled. "Some of the old traditions are still alive." The girl tilted her head in query and the other woman continued. "I've read that it's common on Oriceran to share the food that goes uneaten with animals. It's part of how the different spheres of life interact and find balance. They will do less damage to crops and homes that way."

Cali nodded. "And the stew? Do we always finish it?"

He shook his head. "When we have leftovers that won't be enough or last the next day, I pack it up and take it to a homeless shelter on the east side. Waste not, want not. And if anyone needs good Karma, it's a person who makes their living in the service industry, right?"

She laughed. "You can say that again." She used her final piece of bread to wipe the bowl and ate it with a happy sigh. "So, Emalia, it's clearly not safe for you to be out and about where you can be seen right now."

Zeb frowned. "Why?"

In retrospect, she had to admire his patience in not pressing the scorched and smoky women at his bar for details the moment they'd sat. "I was so busy eating, I forgot I didn't tell you about the evening's adventure." She told him what had happened from start to finish, and his scowl deepened with each passing minute.

At the end, he nodded. "Yes, it's definitely not safe. I agree. We can set up a small bed in the basement if we need to. It's not the fanciest of hotels but it'll serve for a short time."

Cali shook her head. "Thank you for the offer. We might have to do that sometime but I have a different idea for right now. How about you relocate to New Atlantis for a while?" The way Emalia's jaw dropped revealed that she'd surprised the woman, and she laughed. "Why not? I have a big house with no one in it at the moment. I'm sure the wards are as good as anything you'll see here. Although…" She twisted to face Zeb. "How about you come along and examine them? Maybe it's possible to improve or add to what's there."

Her companions looked first at one another, then at her.

Emalia said, "Okay, that's reasonable."

"I'd love to," Zeb stated cheerfully.

She smiled. "Okay, then. Good. I can't do much for Dasante, though. Barton probably won't find a solid enough lead to put useful protection on him. Do you think the magical council might be willing to help?"

The dwarf shrugged. "It wouldn't hurt to ask."

The older woman nodded. "And I'll mention it to Invel. He can argue for it at your side, Zeb."

Cali grinned. "Oh, you have that kind of influence with him, do you?"

Her aunt reddened slightly. "Well, what's the point of having a paramour if you can't rely on them?"

She raised a palm. "That's enough. I don't need to know any more. Not. Another. Word."

They laughed and she caught the look of concern on her boss's face. "What now? Are you worried about being away from the Tavern?"

He slashed his hand in a negative. "No, Janice can handle it."

"Ouch."

A smile flickered on his face but it faded quickly. "I wonder who it was. We absolutely need that answer. Emalia, did you see anything that might give us a hint?"

The woman shrugged. "It began with fire from above, and the Draksa was the only thing I really saw, although…" She trailed off, and despite her desire to find out what was coming next, Cali managed to not interrupt. "I did see what looked like a bright red shoe."

Zeb asked, "A tennis shoe? Converse high tops, maybe?" Cali shot him a look, and he shrugged. "What? I'm hip."

Emalia chuckled. "No. It was shiny."

"A woman's shoe?" the girl asked.

"That seems reasonable."

"So. Since there are only three women I know of who might be after me and one of them isn't likely to visit New Orleans, it leaves the two in charge of the Atlantean gang."

The dwarf nodded. "That sounds right."

"They can't help themselves when it comes to cheating, I guess. It's time for them to learn that their rule-breaking has consequences."

CHAPTER NINE

Her first action after downing her morning coffee was to head into the hallway to knock on Dasante's door. She'd put wards on the landing outside the night before, but her education had included only the most basic ones. Emalia and Zeb had both promised to teach her more, but that would take time she didn't have at the moment. Still, nothing had tripped them, which made her decision to sleep on the couch to be a few seconds closer to the door unnecessary.

She yawned and pounded until he appeared in the doorway, looking as sleepy as she felt. "What?" His voice was thick and croaky.

"I'm checking to make sure you're still alive. Although, to be honest, you do resemble a zombie. You didn't die and then un-die overnight, did you?"

He tilted his head to the side. "Zombies aren't real, are they?"

Cali laughed. "Not the undead ones, at least not as far as I know. I imagine you could take control of someone's mind, though, and turn them into that kind of zombie." She made a mental note to ask about that. She'd heard about necromancers, obviously, but would be the first to admit that her knowledge of the modern-day magical world was limited. Most of her training had been focused on teaching her about her abilities and developing those, but it made sense that she need to learn more than the basics about other things she might have to face.

"Ugh. Gross. No, not dead or undead. Thanks for checking. I'm going back to sleep." The last word melted under a huge yawn as he closed the door, and she laughed as she spun to return to her own apartment. The laugh died at the sight of a note attached to it. Thoughts tumbled out one after the next.

Dammit, they know where I live. Double dammit, my wards failed. Triple dammit, I was ten feet away and didn't sense them.

With a sigh, she pulled the missive off the door and took it inside. Fyre must have sensed her irritation because he was at her side in an instant. She held the envelope up. "Look. A present."

He snorted. "Can we return it? It's sure to be the wrong size."

"Oh, there's no question of that." She used a knife to slit the top and withdrew the paper. It had all the appropriate ritual words, but the most important ones stood out in her vision and she read them aloud. "Four vs Four, tonight at nine, Terisco Machinery."

"What is that?" the Draksa asked.

She tossed the message onto the desk. "An old factory. They made components for some things and assembled others but the business was killed by robotics. It's been closed for as long as I can remember. If this one is anything like the other factories I've seen videos of, it'll make for a challenging battleground, although it probably has high ceilings."

Fyre stretched his neck with a smile. "That will be to our advantage."

"Yeah, theirs too. I bet they bring another Draksa. Or two. Hell, maybe three."

He shook his head. "Most Draksa won't work together without a strong hand to guide them. So two at most with two trainers."

"Really?"

"Yes. We're competitive and only tolerate each other when it's required for survival. Otherwise, not so much."

She grinned. "It must make dating difficult."

He sat and stared lazily at her. "Are you sure you want to know the answer to that?"

"No. Never mind." She raised a hand quickly. "Wow, time is really flying. I'd better take a shower and we need to start getting ready."

The smile on his face suggested that he was laughing at her as she headed down the hallway to the bedroom.

———

A text to Tanyith resulted in a meeting in her hidden bunker a couple of hours before the battle. Cali had spent the time between meditating, resting, and drinking some of the replenishing tea Emalia had insisted she use every day. Her great aunt was safely ensconced in an expensive hotel, courtesy of Invel and the council, until she could take her to New Atlantis and stay for a few days while she acclimated.

She was seated cross-legged on the floor when the portal opened and Tanyith stepped through. He looked at her, gestured at the magical sticks in her hands, and asked, "Are you practicing drums?"

"No." She stuck her tongue out at him. "I'm trying to convince them to become pointy. It's not going well."

"Why?"

When she'd stopped briefly at the Tavern, Zeb had mentioned that Tanyith had come in for a while and that he'd shared the news about Dasante and Emalia with him. "If I'd had something sharp to stab the Draksa with, I might not have had to collapse the building on top of us."

Fyre snorted. "And he would have cooked you when you tried to repeat it."

She sighed. "That's a fair point, but it would still be useful." In truth, she was killing time and doing her best to keep her mind occupied instead of thinking about the battle to come. Tanyith peered around with a confused look on his face, so she shared the bad news. "I've decided not to bring a fourth today. We'll be outnumbered."

He walked to the nearest wall, put his back against it, and slid into a seated position. "Couldn't you find anyone to join us? I'm surprised there isn't a line of volunteers down the street." His voice was sarcastic but warm.

Cali nodded. "Right? The truth is, many people are willing to help, but it feels wrong to put them in harm's way. Emalia? Definitely not. Sensei Ikehara? Maybe, in a pinch, but to send him against magicals without a special weapon he can use to fight them seems like a really bad idea. And Zeb? Well…" She shook her head. "I won't be the one to inspire him to break his vow. He wants to stay retired and I won't try to convince him otherwise."

He grinned. "I could try to convince him."

The Draksa barked a laugh and she said "No. I won't ask. I can't. He's done enough for me already. And, before you say it, yes. Scoppic would probably help, but no, I won't ask the gnome to fight alongside us either."

Tanyith raised his hands and let them fall. "There goes my last good idea."

She smiled. "We're up to it. We can handle them." *Especially now that they've taken away any excuse for holding back by attacking my friends and my family.* "We'll simply have to be faster and smarter than we have been. And on that note, Invel sent a care package with some useful items." She leaned to her left, retrieved the metal box from where it rested on a nearby table, and flipped the lid open.

First, she held up a glass vial that contained a shimmering silver liquid that reminded her of the mercury she'd seen on a tv science show experiment. "This is a potent magical sleep poison. He said it's inert until it touches blood, then it activates. It should take only a minute or two to bring down a normal-sized being." She feinted like she intended to toss the bottle and laughed at the way he flinched. "It's probably best to anoint your Sai before we go and leave the rest here."

He nodded. "That's a good plan. Too bad you don't have a pointy weapon."

"Shut it." She scowled. "Next up are these." She pulled four small transparent spheres from the box, which looked like they were filled with different colors of glitter—red, green, blue, and yellow. Each was about the size and weight of a golf ball. "They have to be thrown hard and will —and I quote—'provide a distraction.' He didn't explain exactly what that meant."

"Well, that's reassuring. Roll me the blue and yellow ones." She complied and he rotated them in a single hand. "Those are both good. Do you have any other fun stuff in there?"

She nodded. "One more thing." She withdrew another two transparent spheres filled with something resembling tiny sparkling shards of diamonds. "Apparently, these will make a Draksa's life especially unhappy. It's essentially broken glass but magical and hard enough to get through the scales on their feet."

"Keep those things far away from me," Fyre commented. "I like my scales the way they are."

Cali nodded. "I'd call this a last resort if we're attacked by an enemy Draksa and have nothing else to defend ourselves with. It's certainly not something to use at the beginning." She rolled one to Tanyith and checked her watch. "We have about half an hour left if we want to be there on time. So yeah, we'd better get to it."

The lockers surrendered additional utility straps that they configured to add the spheres to their uniforms. Tanyith attached them to the front of his weapons belt near his hips. Cali added a gleaming black leather belt specifically to hold hers. They'd discarded the patches that hid the

Leblanc seal, and the outfits looked even more martial than they had before.

"Did you find more of these at the house in New Atlantis?" he asked.

She shook her head. "No, but I haven't explored all the rooms or any of the outbuildings. I plan to finish when I take Emalia there."

He chuckled. "Jenkins will be beside himself with happiness to have a full-time occupant. But I wonder if they weren't produced there, who made them? It'd be interesting to find out if there's someone who does that kind of thing here. Because I won't lie, we'll need every edge we can get, especially if we plan to keep fighting outnumbered."

There was no reluctance in his voice but as much as she feared the answer, she had to check. "You know, you can bail if you want to. Fyre's stuck with me. You're not."

"Hell no. I'm with you to the end. Besides, I still need your help to find that damnable bastard Aiden Walsh."

"Maybe you should give that up."

He smiled. "Maybe you should give this up."

"No chance."

"Well, then. How could I do less?"

She laughed. "You're a moron, you know that?"

His nod was accompanied by a wide grin. "It's been said by others with far more extensive first-hand knowledge than you."

"I guess knowing it is half the battle."

"You're stalling."

Cali sighed. "Yeah, I suppose I am. Final check. Do you

see any problems?" She spread her arms wide and turned in a circle.

"Nope. How about me?" He repeated the process and she also detected nothing amiss.

"Fyre? Are you ready?"

He rose from where he'd sprawled near one wall, stretched like a cat, and raised his rear end high in the air before he walked his paws back to stand properly. "I've been ready for hours. Let's go show these jerks they don't mess with our people."

She nodded resolutely. "I couldn't have said it better myself."

CHAPTER TEN

The portal Tanyith had set up earlier in the day deposited them in front of the factory. Other industrial buildings surrounded it on all sides, mostly abandoned except for a single shipping company that was apparently still in business to judge by the bright blue truck that almost ran them over.

"Maybe position the portal a little farther from the street next time, hmm?" Cali quipped. He gave her a cartoonish scowl and gestured ahead. Large double doors with a broken chain hanging from one handle stood before them. She straightened her back and rolled her neck until a loud crack sounded. "All right. Let's go see what idiots they've brought to fight against us."

In her mind, she added, *Please, let it be the wench in the red shoes.*

Danna Cudon was there, but she wasn't at floor level. A catwalk ran across the outer perimeter of the building about halfway up its three-story height, and several cross pieces connected one side to the other. An audience had found vantage points along them and looked a little smaller than the previous times. Cali shouted, "Your people seem to be losing interest in this. Do you want to call it a day?"

The Atlantean leader laughed. "No, we're good, thanks." She looked as if she'd dressed to impress with perfect hair and an almost funereal black suit offset by a scarlet shirt, tie, and shoes. "Would you like to forfeit? I can offer you a quick death."

"Hard pass." She whispered to Tanyith, "It was worth a shot, right?"

He nodded. "They're not smart enough to give up. But I've gotta say, I'm not a fan of this setup."

She couldn't have agreed more. Heavy pieces of equipment cluttered the area, arranged in no obvious pattern. Keeping an enemy at range would be difficult. The high ceiling offered an opportunity to anyone able to fly, and it would be too hopeful to believe the other side hadn't selected at least one airborne fighter.

Cudon interrupted her train of thought as she called, "I only see three of you. The note was clear that this was a four-on-four battle." An expression of false shock and concern appeared on her face. "Don't tell me you've run out of allies already, Caliste. Surely you have more than two beings left on this planet who care for you." She finished with a wide grin.

Well, that's a big clue about who attacked Emalia and tried to kill Dasante. She didn't imagine the woman had accomplished both on her own but she had almost certainly been involved since taunting her about it brought her such pleasure.

"Not at all," she replied. "Based on the previous fights, we calculated that we're worth at least six of yours. It seemed unfair to bring more."

The other woman's laugh sounded forced. "Your over-confidence will prove to be your undoing. Are you prepared?"

Cali frowned. *Won't we see our opponents before the fight starts? I guess that might not be a rule.* She turned to Tanyith, who nodded and then to Fyre, who growled eagerly. Aggression and confidence flowed to her over their mental connection. *All righty then.* "Let's do it, wench."

The grin that she so desperately wanted to slap off Cudon's face appeared again. "Let the battle commence," she shouted, and two roars echoed in response. The first was from the crowd above, who punctuated the yell by stamping their feet on the metal catwalks. That wasn't worrisome.

The second, though, emanated from floor level and sounded like a seriously ticked off lion—if lions were the size of elephants. She shook her head. "It's always an adventure with these scumbags. Split up, stay safe, and use magic from the start. Maybe that will give us a momentary benefit of surprise, anyway."

They nodded and Tanyith eased to the left while Fyre took to the air. She moved right under the cover of machinery, thankful for once that she wasn't model-tall.

The Draksa soared over the factory floor and searched for

the four opponents that were doubtless already in position to attack his teammates.

Not if I have anything to say about it. He located the enormous creature that had emitted the roar and growled deep in the back of his throat. His turn in that direction was cut off by the sudden appearance of another Draksa that arrowed up from directly below. It was bigger than him, and the light glinted off its fully metallic scales to mark it as male. They were pure ebony except at the pointed tips, where a slightly lighter outline resembled an arrow pointing back along its body.

He rolled to evade the slashing claws of his foe, only to discover that the attack had been calculated to force him into the handler's line of fire. A burst of lightning streaked from floor level and wreathed him in pinpoints of agony. He folded his wings and dropped to land hard but mostly uninjured. His scales would stand up to almost any harm for at least a brief period.

Entirely focused, he considered the angles and scurried to where the one who'd attacked him had been. His gaze moved constantly, alert to any warning that the other Draksa attacked again.

Speed will be everything in this fight. Fortunately, I'm the fastest being I know.

Tanyith crept carefully from cover to cover and searched for any sign of motion or of an opponent. Verbal abuse rained from above but seemed to all be general insults rather than anything specific that might be a cause to claim cheating.

As if they haven't cheated at every turn. Anger surged through him, and he shook his head to clear it. Since the trip to New Atlantis, he'd found his patience seemed to wear out rapidly. It was doubtless because he vehemently disliked being obligated to the Malniets. That, plus the ache in his back that even sips of healing potion didn't seem to banish, kept him cranky.

And now, I need someone to take it out on. A thin grin stretched his lips when he saw the tip of a boot protrude from behind a piece of equipment ahead and to the left. He focused his attention on his magic, drew it forth, and held it, increasing the pressure with each passing second. *I gotta go as far as I can for this to work.* Finally, when he could no longer restrain the growing power, he threw it forward.

The force blast pounded into the huge machine. With a squeal of broken fasteners and sliding metal, the object slid along the floor and away from him but failed to topple as he'd hoped.

Damn it, I should have hit higher. A figure sprawled in the open space beside it but rolled out of sight too quickly for his follow-up force bolts to intercept. The microphone pinned to his uniform collar carried his voice to the flesh-colored earpiece Cali wore. "I found one, probably an enforcer. I'll take care of him."

Cali nodded, even though he couldn't see it. "Got it. No contact here yet, although it feels like Fyre is fighting." The microphones and earpieces were part of a set of four she'd found among the spy gear.

Four. Mom, Dad, Atreo, and I. She closed her eyes and allowed herself a moment of regret for what could have been, then jerked her attention to the present. A blur above had caught her notice moments before and she attributed it to the flying creature she'd expected. The emotions from her dragon lizard partner were the same as when he'd faced another Draksa, so she presumed that was what it was. A familiar crackle suggested its breath attack was electricity.

She hated being on the receiving end of lightning. It burned, cut, and plain hurt. For all those reasons, she looked forward to adding the magic to her offensive arsenal to give her foes a taste of their own medicine. Her eyes narrowed at the sight of a thin passage between two pieces of high equipment ahead. It blocked her view and would leave her vulnerable while she went through.

Decisions, decisions.

Before she got too swept up in her internal debate to go through or around, she decided to go over. She used a blast of force magic to vault the pieces and remained alert for the enemy Draksa. She didn't see it but she did notice the flying net as it hurtled toward her. Lightning licked along the mesh, and she realized instantly that it wasn't rope with electricity on it but a web formed of the electrical magic itself.

She battered it with a burst of force to send it off course and had a moment of satisfaction before another roar sounded, this one from much closer than before. Her gaze snapped down when a giant form knocked aside pieces of equipment as it closed on the position she had chosen for her landing.

Holy hell. How did a crab get so damned huge?

Fyre broke out into the open and located the enemy handler, who magically retrieved a lightning net from the air. She was clad in what looked like plates made of shell over a layer of leather. The brown base and beige pieces complemented one another and her light hair was braided in a single strand that fell to the middle of her back. He grinned at the woman's distraction and took a deep breath as he performed his quiet serpentine slither to close the distance. When he was close enough, he directed a blast of frost at her.

The other Draksa intercepted his attack with a barrage of lightning that suffused and melted his magical assault, which resulted in its handler suffering nothing more than a cold, soaking shower. He launched another blast of frost, this time at the other dragon lizard, but again, their magics met and were rendered ineffective.

Claws and teeth, then.

He drove forward on the assumption that his foe would expect a less direct approach. When the other Draksa lowered its head to protect its vulnerable neck and eyes, Fyre leapt over it, scraped his claws down its back, and landed in a sprint toward the handler.

His airborne opponent bellowed and thrashed, and its thick tail slapped him into the air. It was a short flight that ended with a loud impact against a heavy piece of manufacturing gear. He landed hard, momentarily dazed, and when his senses returned, both the Draksa and its partner closed on him. The latter swung the net in one hand and grasped a trident poised to throw in the other.

As she landed and frantically avoided the snapping claws, Cali yelled, "Guys, it's a giant crab and its pincers look really damn sharp. Other than summoning an immense hammer, how do I defeat this thing?"

The connection with Fyre was filled with battle emotions, so she couldn't get a read on his response. Tanyith merely laughed. "Giant leg-cracker thingy, maybe?" He sounded out of breath and gave a small yelp. "I'm gonna have to get back to you."

She ducked and rolled under another swipe of the beast's front appendages and fired a force bolt that struck it squarely in the face, hoping there were eyes in there that she might damage. It didn't seem to be affected in the least, so she tried flames instead—the largest cone she could summon targeted the same place. Aside from turning its rainbow-hued shell a slightly brighter shade, that also failed to accomplish anything notable.

The beast scuttled ahead and eight turquoise legs propelled it forward while the two that ended in sharp black tips reached for her. She shook her head.

I'll never be able to watch the Little Mermaid again. Things from Under the Sea should bloody well stay there.

CHAPTER ELEVEN

Tanyith closed on the Atlantean enforcer, who had found his feet by the time he located him again. The man wore the crab-inspired armor he'd encountered on a previous opponent, but his wasn't in natural shades. Instead, the hard shell was painted with images of combat. He frowned. "Before we try to kill each other, what's up with the pictures?"

His foe grinned and spun the long spear at his side from its attack position to vertical and thumped the blunt bottom against the ground. "Each is a battle I have fought and won. I come from a family of warriors, and someday in the distant future, my armor shall join theirs to tell of our legacy."

"You seem…uh, fairly accomplished."

The man nodded and the portion of his face visible beneath the half-helm that covered the upper part revealed a smile. "Indeed. Soon, I'll enter the trials to become one of the Empress's personal guards." He said the words with deep reverence, whether for the battles to come or the potential for serving the monarch, Tanyith had no idea.

"I'm sorry to hear that. Your loss today will certainly be a black mark on your record. You could leave, though. That wouldn't count as a defeat, merely an intelligent decision."

The enforcer laughed. "Enough conversation. I must kill you quickly so I can engage the others before my inferiors dispatch them." He lowered the spear and advanced, looking as if being struck by the giant piece of machinery earlier hadn't affected him at all.

Damn it. He drew his Sai and charged to meet him, hoping a surprise speed attack might get past the man's defenses. *One cut, that's all I need to knock him out.* He was forced onto the defensive as the enforcer used the length of his weapon and stabbed it forward on the line of his approach. Tanyith swung his right-hand weapon up and out, caught the metal point in the guard, and moved it away. He couldn't get close enough to attack and still control the weapon, though, and when he released the spear to lunge ahead, his foe pivoted and smacked him with the shaft.

The blow caught his shoulder and knocked him aside. The short wind-up lacked enough force to do any damage but delivered enough to provide his opponent a moment to get outside his daggers' range again. He considered hurling his weapons in the hope that he might achieve a lucky hit, but they weren't balanced for throwing and he hadn't really been all that lucky of late.

He set his feet and waited for the man's next attack.

Fyre charged the enemy Draksa in the hope that the assault would keep the handler from launching the trident. Casting the net would require her to twist awkwardly across her body, which would compromise the aim. That part of the plan worked, but he received a full blast of electricity from his winged counterpart. He growled through the pain as he twisted his head to breathe ice over the woman, but she dove aside to avoid the attack.

A claw raked along his side and sliced through several scales before he could take to the air to escape it. As he flapped his wings to gain altitude, he exhaled another cone of frost at the enemy Draksa, who defended with his own breath weapon. The lightning net spiraled in and Fyre plummeted in a shallow dive to avoid it. The evasion made him lose sight of his foes but revealed the giant creature menacing Cali.

He coated it with frost, but while its shell immediately became rimmed with ice, it didn't appear to hinder the beast. The crab continued to close on her as he circled, but his attention was ripped away by another flurry of lightning from the enemy Draksa that passed under his extended wing. The dire need to end his own battle to assist with the creature was a sudden and powerful pressure, but he pushed the worry aside.

I can't afford to be distracted, not against two.

They had obviously trained together, as his effort to dodge a lightning blast from below put him in the path of one from the other dragon lizard that scorched the scales on his belly. Even though his body would repair them quickly, the successive attacks risked a strike against them while they were weak, which would probably be fatal in this kind of fight. Outdoors, he would simply work to draw them away from one another, but there wasn't enough room for that to be an option in the current battle.

Only a single solution offered a reasonable chance of success, and even though he didn't like the idea, his body already shifted to make the attempt before the logical part of his mind could override the plan.

Cali summoned her sticks and raced toward the crab, dodged between the grasping claws, and drove her weapons into where she thought its face should be. The flesh there gave a little, more than a shell would have, but the beast seemed not to care. It scuttled far faster than she would have believed possible and snapped at her from both sides. She vaulted upward on a force blast and landed six feet away from her opponent, but it had already resumed its attack.

Damn it, how am I supposed to get through that shell? Maybe I can crush the bastard with something?

She turned and sprinted through a slalom of equipment, hoping to buy time. The sound of crashing metal behind her confirmed that the crab pursued. She trickled power into her muscles, heart, and lungs to increase her speed to remain ahead of her foe. The sight of the jeering audience overhead triggered the idea of dropping a catwalk or three on the creature, but she rejected it as potentially ineffective and definitely outside her comfort range. Killing someone who tried to kill her was one thing. She didn't like it but she'd do it if required. To simply kill the other gang members while they watched wasn't an option.

A single image stood out among them—the grinning face of Danna Cudon. Okay, maybe she could make an exception for her. She slid to cross under the center portion of a large piece of equipment and emerged facing in the other direction. The crab grasped the multi-ton metal machine and ripped it from the floor. In the instant the machinery was held high, she assaulted it with a full-strength burst of force and hurled it out of the creature's hold to land on its shell. The machine bounced and tumbled off the side, and the giant crustacean stopped in its tracks.

Go down, you bastard.

Cali's moment of hope was brief as the beast scuttled toward her with another deafening roar and forced her to run again. Since when, she wondered desperately, did damn crabs roar?

Fyre accepted the lightning blast the handler fired from her trident and wondered idly if the magic came from the weapon or was channeled through it. The attack scoured his side, penetrated a weakened scale, and stabbed into his flesh. He locked his jaw against the pain and knew it was a small precursor to a larger portion to come.

He tucked his wings to send him into a dive and his momentum careened him into the enemy Draksa, who twisted in the air to meet him belly to belly. His foe's claws ripped at him, dislodged a few scales, and tore others free. The continued assault slashed into his flesh and he screamed in fury. But, he reminded himself grimly, he would only have to endure the attack for a couple of moments more.

A shout from below signaled the handler's recognition of her danger, but their velocity made it too late. Fyre thrust his adversary into her as she tried to evade, and the speed with which they collided drove her into the concrete floor beneath them with enough force to kill her. He tumbled away from his enemy, scrambled to avoid a follow-up attack, and trailed scarlet blood. His foe uttered a keening wail at the loss of its partner, and although they were enemies, he felt deep sympathy for the creature. He couldn't imagine losing Cali and wouldn't even allow his thoughts to travel in that direction.

When the enemy Draksa raised its gaze to him, he saw what that level of anguish looked like. Its eyes held no sanity and only pain. With a growl punctuating each step, the mad dragon lizard stalked closer.

Cali cut to her left to avoid leading the giant creature toward where Tanyith had gone. A flood of satisfaction from Fyre had been followed by a surge of concern, and a matching emotion coursed through her on his behalf.

"Stay safe, buddy," she sent and said, "This stupid crab shell is impenetrable." No reply came, and she decided that where before she thought she probably hated the factory as a battlefield, she was now certain of it.

She emerged in an empty space that looked like it might have been a loading dock or storage area to judge by the large garage doors on the walls. The crustacean bulldozed through a moment later and she turned to face it and launched cones of flame from each hand, the ineffective Escrima sticks in their bracelet form again. The beast walked through the fire, seemingly unconcerned. She growled a curse, followed by a shouted, "What is it with you? Go away, stupid beast."

The monster responded with a swipe of its claw that she dropped prone to avoid, only to have the other one descend at incredible speed. She rolled to dodge it and stopped abruptly when the first appeared in her path. They started to sweep in as she scrambled to her feet and used a force blast to elevate above the appendages.

Unfortunately, her enemy had seen that trick already. With a skitter and a swipe of its claw, it intercepted and redirected her flight to catapult her into the wall. Her hastily summoned cocoon shield absorbed part of the initial impact but less of her fall. She groaned around the pain that flooded through her chest and the agony of the leg that had broken when she'd landed with the limb twisted beneath her. Her fingers scrabbled at her thigh pouch and retrieved a healing potion. She popped the top, drained the vial in a single motion, and scrambled away on her hands and knees. The forced movement of the only partially restored leg dragged a scream from deep in her chest.

Cali summoned a wall of flame to block her adversary's

view of her and crawled to the cover of nearby equipment. Hopefully, she could finish her recovery before it plowed through the obstacles and found her.

Tanyith darted in again, slapped the spear aside, and flicked his blade at the man's face. Exactly as he'd done the previous two times, the enforcer pulled his head back and out of the way, which caused the drug-coated Sai to miss. This time, though, his enemy didn't disengage but stepped forward to bring his helmet down in a violent head butt.

He dropped to the ground to avoid the attack, his balance insufficient to dodge to either side. His foe whipped the spear around his head and drove it down, and Tanyith pushed himself back and spread his legs wide. The point stabbed into the concrete floor an inch from his right knee, and he rolled into a backward somersault while his enemy wrenched it free.

The most annoying part of the fight wasn't the man's greater reach, although he didn't particularly enjoy that. Nor was it the armor that had turned aside several attempts to pierce it, which was also frustrating. No, the truly infuriating thing was the confident grin that never left his face, as if he was no threat at all and merely an inconvenience.

Thankfully, the man irritated him enough to increase his determination to defeat him. He tossed one Sai in the air, fired a force burst at his adversary's legs, and caught the blade on the way down. His foe conjured a shield to block and shook his head. "Please. If that's the best you can do, you should simply lie down. I'll make it quick."

"You should lie down," he muttered and repeated the process with both hands. The enforcer shifted the shield to intercept one and leaned out of the way of the other, which allowed the attack to pass unimpeded, slam into a piece of machinery behind him, and shatter the plastic case with a loud crack.

That gave him an idea, and he smiled as he caught the hilts of the drugged blades cleanly.

Okay, pal. It's time to fight dirty.

CHAPTER TWELVE

The potion finished its work and Cali groaned with relief as her broken bones mended and wounded flesh healed. She took the energy draught from her thigh pouch and downed the thick liquid. Her swallows matched cadence with the wrenching of metal from where she'd last seen the crab, and it was only a moment more before the monster thrust the heavy equipment out of the way to clear a path to her.

"Okay, shell-face. It's time to get serious." While she'd been reluctant to put Invel's gifts to use unnecessarily, there was no question that she needed to try something different. She lowered her right hand, retrieved the two distractions on her belt, and performed her best baseball pitch to lob the initial one at the crab's apparently eyeless face and the other at its feet a moment later.

The first struck and exploded into a fine mist that appeared to stick to the surface of the beast. It made a sound resembling a sneeze and shook violently, and she would have sworn the creature seemed confused. The second globe struck and a wall of glitter rose into the air and sparkled brilliantly to create another sight-blocking barrier between her and her target. She sprinted to her right, hoping to circle and attack from the rear while it was otherwise occupied. Another sneeze came from the opposite side of the sparkling curtain.

Interesting choices, Invel. Something tells me your background isn't strategy and tactics, though.

She crept through the maze of equipment and smiled when she found herself directly behind the beast as it poked the glimmering wall tentatively with its claws. She drew on her magic and channeled it into her fists for what she hoped would be the strongest human crab-mallet ever.

Fyre had never seen one of his kind move so fast. He darted to the side and rolled as the enemy Draksa plowed through the space he'd occupied and snapped and growled in fury when it missed. The creature had clearly been driven beyond comprehension by the death of its handler and was now far more dangerous because of the loss.

He vaulted and flapped his wings to dodge his foe's next attack, a wicked blast of lightning that followed a sliding, scrambling turn. The dragon lizard had abandoned any sense of defensive self-preservation, but its furious attacks left little opening for a counter assault. Fyre dove and swooped among the broken equipment as his opponent raced after him, then looped up and over a catwalk in the vague hope that the audience might feel itself at risk and intervene. Instead, they cheered his foe and simply ducked to avoid its claws as it sped past.

Conscious of the blind rage that drove his adversary, he hurtled toward the far wall, descended to increase his speed, and pulled up to barrel-roll and engage his enemy. The other Draksa was much closer than he'd expected, and they traded long scratches that drew blood from each other. Their matching angry bellows echoed off the metal walls of the facility. They both halted their momentum with a rapid beating of wings and turned to face one another again. His breath weapon emerged an instant before his foe's, and they collided to create a rain shower that covered a third of the factory floor.

Fyre searched for an option, something in the environment to use against his enemy, but found nothing. He dove and spun and pushed himself to top speed to gain distance from the other Draksa. He flashed over Cali, who fought a giant crab, and he growled in frustration.

She needs my help, which means this jerk has to go.

Tanyith whipped one of Invel's globes from his belt and hoped fervently that the distraction would be useful against the smug enforcer. It connected with the man's knee and exploded in a cloud of blue metallic confetti that saturated the air around him. The sight inspired a second diversion, and he lobbed the sphere filled with crystal shards in a gentle arc at his foe. A force blast followed immediately to shatter the container and propel the sharp pieces into the man's face.

The Atlantean recoiled with a shout of pain as the tiny shrapnel pierced his flesh, then growled and surged into an attack, leading with the spear.

You bastard. You're not so smug anymore, are you? His previously handsome visage was now a mess of torn and bleeding skin. Tanyith had hoped his eyes might be vulnerable but naturally, his enemy was too smart for that and his half-helm protected them. But both of those attacks were only preludes to the real one and intended only as a distraction from his true plan.

He reached out with his magic and took hold of the pieces broken off nearby machines as they battled. There were a number of them, from baseball-sized to barely more than dust, and he hurled all of them at his opponent from two directions at once. The projectiles battered him and drew curses and snarls as he raised his arms to protect himself and spun the spear to deflect a particularly large chunk.

The attempt to defend himself created a momentary opening, which was all Tanyith needed to slash his blade across the side of the man's neck. He could have made a deep cut but he pulled the blow at the last moment and backpedaled. The enforcer spun in a rage but managed only two steps before he dropped to one knee with a look of confusion on his ravaged face. He remained vertical for several seconds before unconsciousness toppled him into a motionless heap.

He snatched the spear up in case the man woke before the fight was over—he really did not want to deal with the weapon in his hands again—and ran to where crashes, bangs, and yells marked the place where his partner was fighting. He could hear her muttering over the comm, and answered, "I'm on my way. Hang in there."

When the power had built fully, Cali raised both her fists high and brought them down while she imagined a mammoth hammer striking the crab. The beast fell beneath the impact, and she had a moment of hope before it staggered upright again. She shouted insults in a fury and looked around her for something to use against the seemingly impenetrable shell. At this point, she almost believed that pulling the catwalks down seemed like the only viable option and had already begun to consider how best to do so when Tanyith appeared in the corner of her vision.

That was good, but what was better was the spear in his hand. "Give me that," she said and he tossed it toward her. She twisted, caught it, and spun the weapon. Its balance was perfect, which made it no more difficult to handle than the jo staff her sticks combined to create.

And this one is pointy. She whipped her head back to get strands of hair out of her face and grinned at the monster. "Okay, you bastard. Zeb's gonna have crabmeat in the stew tomorrow."

She poured magic into her muscles and organs and surged forward to see what her new weapon could accomplish against the oversized seafood dinner that once again snapped its claws at her.

Fyre saw the narrow lane between the equipment and knew he could make it with only a little luck. He dove toward the floor, pulled up an instant before impact, and made a sharp left turn. Lightning from his pursuer struck the wall of equipment to the right and shattered one large piece into several smaller ones that pinwheeled in every direction. A chunk caught him a glancing blow but he barely noticed it as he curved into the open area he'd aimed for.

The lane stretched in front of him but navigating it would require all his flying and evasive abilities. His wings flapped furiously to gain as much speed as he could before the available space narrowed. He swooped low and twisted to the right, then had to swing to the left to pass between a broken piece on the floor and a tall beam that crossed the path. A furious growl behind him as he gained distance indicated that the bigger Draksa proved to be a less proficient flyer.

Yes, this will work.

He saw the giant crab to his right as he rocketed past but had no attention to spare. The thoughts from Cali were all aggressive, so he was confident that she wasn't in imminent danger. His all-out speed brought the moment he'd waited for much quicker than expected. He pulled up to avoid the wall, careened through a square of hanging beams, and twisted to let his momentum carry him toward the ceiling. At the perfect moment, he exhaled his frost breath—not at the Draksa but at the girders to spread a barrier across between them. His pursuer pounded into the ice without slowing and although the impact didn't stop him, it did kill his forward progress.

From there, the rest was simple. Fyre dove and latched on to the other Draksa to drive him into the floor below with all the power he possessed. The impact crushed the vital organs and his adversary didn't even twitch once he released him. Satisfied, he launched into flight to help his friends.

Cali spun the spear as she ran a circle around the crab and her magical speed kept her safely ahead of its wickedly barbed claws. She was testing the beast to see how well it could track her while she gained momentum for the next part of her plan. When she thought she had learned its movements, she gave her legs an extra burst of power and jumped. She landed on the side of its shell and slipped, then caught her balance and leapt again, aiming for its front.

Her feet found purchase, and she channeled all her magically enhanced strength and the power of her momentum into a downward thrust of the spear. The weapon penetrated the shell and stabbed deep into the creature, which bucked under her feet. Tanyith landed beside her and fired lightning into the open wound as she yanked the blade free. She vaulted off and its thrashing limbs forced her to use the weapon to block as she repositioned. "Tanyith, get down here," she called. "I need your help."

He complied and she asked, "Can you fling that monster into the air?" He frowned but nodded and she grinned. She'd seen the Draksa circling above and the sight had inspired a plan. "Trust me. Fyre, when it comes up, you hammer the bastard down again. On three." She counted, poured magic into her body, then dashed forward as she announced the final number. The creature rose about five feet as Tanyith achieved something that probably wouldn't have worked if the beast hadn't already been focused on the agony from the wound on its back. Her speed took her all the way across the gap while it was in the air with no problem.

She spun to watch as Fyre came down hard on the crab. She'd left the spear positioned below it with the point up and wedged at the shell's lowest point. The Draksa drove the monster onto the weapon and the enormous crustacean shrieked, thrashed, and collapsed to twitch and writhe for a few moments.

Cali looked at the Atlantean leader. "Get down here, witch. Let's chat."

It took a minute or so for Danna Cudon to make her way to the floor from the catwalk, and by the time she appeared, the condescending smile was on her face again. "Well done, Caliste. You continue to prove to be a worthy enemy." She raised an eyebrow. "Perhaps you'd consider giving up your opposition to us and joining our effort instead? We only desire the best for magicals in New Orleans. You could be a part of making that happen."

She shook her head. "Stop talking. I get a request, remember?"

The Atlantean laughed. "Is that your boon? That I stop talking?"

"Ha, ha, ha. No. Here's what I want. From here on out,

my friend Dasante is off-limits to you, as are any humans I associate with. This garbage is between us. Got it?"

"That's a big ask."

She shrugged. "I defeated your four with my three. I'm sure that counts for something in the convoluted rules." Her voice lowered into something close to a growl. "And maybe consider it less a reward for my victory than a way to avoid having me hunt and kill each of you individually for messing with my friends."

The enemy leader clucked her tongue. "Look at you, protecting the fragile humans. You are truly a caring soul. For now." Her tone suggested it wouldn't last.

"Do we have a deal?"

Cudon nodded. "Accepted. We won't target your precious human pets. We can't speak for the Zatoras or the Malniets, of course, or anyone not in our gang."

Cali ground her teeth at the unsubtle hint. "If I trace anything to you, rituals be damned, I'll take your organization apart. Beginning with you, fire-starter." The other woman's grin was all the confirmation she needed. "Now, get your people out of here."

It was petty, perhaps, but she watched with her arms folded while the Atlanteans departed to ensure that they remembered they had left at her command because they'd lost. Fyre stood on her left and Tanyith on her right to oversee the procession in silence. When they were alone again, the Draksa snorted. "They won't behave. Nice try, though."

She nodded. "It wasn't about making them behave. It was about being able to force the Empress to turn against them—or at least leave them unsupported if they break the rules."

Her partner shook his head. "When they break the rules."

"Yeah. Tell your girlfriend to be careful and to keep an eye on Sienna and anyone else important to you. I'm reasonably sure Dasante's safe but beyond that, I won't count on anything."

CHAPTER THIRTEEN

S henni, Empress of New Atlantis, resisted the urge to scream at the woman who knelt at the bottom of the stairs leading to the dais her throne stood on. The formality of Usha's reception—rather than a conversation in her private office—would be signal enough of her displeasure. Her elite guards were positioned to either side of her subordinate, an obvious threat and additional message.

Her robes of state were another indication that the leader of the Atlantean gang in New Orleans had transgressed. She wore the scarlet undergarment that reached her chin and required her to lean forward to look down. It gave her a haughty and dismissive demeanor that was exacerbated by the deep-blue top layer, which was dark and foreboding and long enough to trail behind her when she walked. They were the kind of impractical items that communicated one's ability to have others take action on their behalf.

The report of the failed assault on Caliste Leblanc's

friend was bad. Discovering that the child's only known relative had also been attacked was worse. And the fact that the matriarch of House Leblanc had won another ritual battle while voluntarily outnumbered rose to the level of insult.

Doubtless as the little witch intended.

Usha had accepted full responsibility for the actions of her subordinates in each of the matters, but the Empress knew one could only work with what one had. It was the ultimate limitation on power, the need to rely on others. She had researchers working on that problem from multiple angles but so far had not found a viable solution.

She kept her face impassive and decided that the woman needed to pass a few more minutes in silent submission to ensure the weight of her disapproval was properly communicated. Her seneschal was nearby, as always, and she flicked her gaze to the left to meet Gwyn's. She activated the telepathic connection between them and sent, "She seems truly regretful."

The other woman's head dipped in a slight nod before she schooled herself into immobility while she responded in thought. "Indeed, Empress. Usha has never given any indication that she feels anything other than complete love and dedication toward you. The failures of those she leads are unfortunate, as was the failure of the enforcer you sent."

"The child is proving to be more of a challenge than expected."

Gwyn's pale lips twisted in a hint of a smile. "The same could be said of House Leblanc for its entire history."

"True enough." She let the channel between them fall

away. After several more minutes, she said aloud, "Usha, rise." The woman flowed smoothly to her feet and showed no sign of discomfort.

She could have two broken legs and would display nothing. Her subordinate's strength of will set her apart from most of the other individuals in her life and earned her privileges and opportunities that others would never receive. *Including second chances.*

Still, this rebuke needed to be formal. "You are my trusted lieutenant, but these reports of ongoing failure by your people are troublesome. Henceforth, do not be reluctant to request what you need from Gwyn. Pride is of no value in the battle for the soul of New Atlantis. While Caliste Leblanc may be a problem that cannot be solved on the surface, you must succeed in all the other tasks you have been given. And, of course, continue to press the girl to join us or attempt to remove her from the equation."

Her subordinate's voice brimmed with the knowledge of her failure. "Yes, Empress. It will be done."

"See that it is. You are dismissed from our presence." Her seneschal swept forward to escort the woman from the throne room. When it was only Shenni and her guards, she rose and descended the stairs slowly, deep in thought. By the time she reached the bottom, she had a new plan. She addressed the guard on her right. "Send word for my seneschal to attend me in the office in an hour." The man nodded, and both enforcers escorted her to her chambers, which were guarded by yet another two. A servant stood nearby, and the Empress ordered, "Draw a bath. I need to wash the stress of this day away."

Gwyn awaited her in the office and stood with her back to the main door when Shenni entered through the hidden one at the rear of the room. She sat behind the desk and gestured for her subordinate to sit in the chair across from her. With a small smile, she asked, "How did Usha take it?"

The other woman answered the smile with her own. "Very well, Empress. She has requested support in several areas and seems fully committed to accomplishing the tasks you have given her."

"Good. Everyone needs a little reinforcement now and again. These short-term failures may turn out to be to our long-term benefit." Her seneschal didn't reply, and she considered her idea once more before she shared it.

It's a good plan. Chaos to my enemies.

"I think we need to start putting pressure on Matriarch Leblanc from this side of the water. Please arrange for Patriarch Wymarc to see me."

The other woman grinned. "The most beautiful man in the Nine? It would be my decided pleasure, Empress."

She nodded. "And hopefully, young Caliste's, as well."

The arrangements had been made for her guest to join her for dinner, a privilege reserved for very, very few. She tried to separate her life, with dinner as the demarcation point where the public Empress became the private Shenni.

But some needs require sacrifices. When he entered, she

couldn't help but smile. *And some sacrifices really aren't that great a burden, after all.*

He had olive skin and lush hair that fell to his shoulders in soft waves. She'd heard servants describe his cheekbones as sharp enough to slice a heart open and couldn't argue with the assessment. Everything else in his face was in perfect alignment, and the body revealed by the tight trousers and perfectly tailored shirt he wore was undeniably powerful. In his early twenties, he was younger than her by a decade and a half or so and still retained a palpable sense of self-appreciation.

The product of a sheltered upbringing, to be sure, but he certainly is a pretty ornament.

His strength was visible in the way he moved as Wymarc Jehenel crossed the room and knelt beside where she sat at the head of the table. She nodded in acknowledgment. "Sit. We have matters to discuss." She gestured to the chair on her left at the small rectangular table in the private dining room. At most, the space would accommodate five as it was unseemly for someone to dine at the opposite end facing her. Tonight, it was set for two with an expensive turquoise tablecloth, fine china plates with a golden filigree—discovered in a shipwreck—and matching golden silverware. No knives were present and all food would arrive pre-cut. An empath, one of the rarer magical specialties, was behind the wall to her right, along with her most proficient spellcaster and two guards with mounted crossbows. At any sign of aggression, they would eliminate the man.

The first course, a variety of seafood in a thin savory broth, arrived in the hands of her seneschal, who doubled as a server for these events. Her food tasters would have tried it before it was allowed into the room with her, and it would have been examined for hostile magic as well. Her layers of security were mostly invisible but undeniably necessary.

Wymarc ventured small talk and she listened politely, but she had little real interest in his life beyond the formative details. His parents had died young, leaving the most direct family line with no other progeny to take the role. He had spent his childhood and teens in the care of more distant members of the house, who had unexpectedly failed to eliminate him, and had taken the title of patriarch when he turned nineteen. In the three years since, he had done nothing of note beyond maintaining his impressively good looks.

Shenni let him lead the conversation through the soup and the vegetable course that followed it, then took control as the main dish, lobster and crab exquisitely grilled and flavored, arrived. It was one of her favorites and always her go-to recipe when she was seeking something from a guest. The spices used were from the surface and unavailable anywhere in New Atlantis other than the palace. "So, Wymarc, how fares House Jehenel?"

"Excellently, Empress. The plans my parents put into place before their deaths have served us well and I have seen no reason to change them."

"And the future of your line?"

He smiled, an edge of flirtation in the tilt of his lips. "To be determined, Empress. I have not yet found the right partner." His voice betrayed him and she could hear the desire in it. Inwardly, she laughed. Outwardly, she nodded seriously.

"Your misfortune thus far in that area might work toward our mutual benefit, however." She paused long enough for him to get his hopes up, then continued. "How did you find our newest matriarch?"

He was too polished to let his disappointment show and covered it by taking a bite of his food and chewing thoughtfully. With meticulous manners, he dabbed his lips with a linen napkin and replied, "Young. Headstrong, certainly. Unpolished. But there is no mistaking that she is a Leblanc." He said it with a hint of derision and she laughed.

"So, she's been the subject of conversation among the Nine, then? That is interesting—and, of course, appropriate. She is a new variable, to be sure." He wasn't old enough to have formed an opinion about the Leblancs before they'd left New Atlantis, which meant someone had told him of their history. *Alliances are already forming against her, then, or at least with an eye toward using her.* "Do you have a sense of her loyalties?"

"No, Empress. None. Her time in the city was too short to gain any useful information about her."

Shenni nodded. "How would you go about doing so?" She put a hint of intrigue in her words, and he leaned forward involuntarily in response.

"The oldest ways are the best ways, Empress. I would be a friend, an ally, and eventually, a lover. Her secrets would be open to me in no time." His entendre was clumsy but apt.

"Indeed." She smiled. "That seems like a good plan. And

were you to learn things, who would you share them with? The other houses?"

"Only if you wished it. Otherwise, only you."

She chuckled. "So dutiful, so appropriate." She shook her head. "Now really, which other houses are allied with yours? I must know where the knowledge will flow if I am to help you gain it."

To his credit, he didn't look abashed at her words. *He has some steel in his spine, then.*

"I am most closely aligned with houses Terriau, Oubre, and of course Rivette, Empress, all of whom support you unreservedly, as do I."

"Excellent." *Partial truth. While my own former house naturally supports me, Oubre is slightly less committed and Terriau is filled with opportunists. Exactly like House Jehenel.*

When they finished their meal, she signaled for dessert and tea. She tasted the decadently light vanilla cake and pronounced it delicious, and her guest seconded the opinion, as he would, of course. "Let us enter into an accord. I shall provide you with an excuse to spend time with young Caliste. You will do whatever you can to discover her secrets and report them to me before you share them with your allies. The decision of what stays between us and what may go further rests with me."

He nodded. "I am willing to accept that bargain, Empress, the moment I know how my house and I will be rewarded for it."

She laughed out loud. "Oh, you are bold—very bold, Wymarc. But not entirely unreasonable. How about this? When you do finally select a mate to bear your children, the palace will match whatever dowry is paid by the family." It was a classic Atlantean suggestion as it included an edge of competition and challenge. Would he choose the best partner or the one who would bring him the greatest treasure? Or somehow find someone who accomplished both? It would be enjoyable to watch it play out.

He matched her laughter. "That is quite appropriate, Empress. On behalf of House Jehenel, I accept."

She sent a mental touch to her seneschal and asked her to enter. When she did so, Shenni described the arrangement and ordered it to be put into writing and formally sealed. The woman nodded and escorted her dinner guest from the room. The Empress waved as he departed but her mind was already involved with the next part of her plan.

Now, how best to get Caliste Leblanc into a position to fall into dear Wymarc's strong arms?

CHAPTER FOURTEEN

Cali shouted in anger as she tried and failed to block the sword with the magical jo staff composed of her combined sticks. It caught her hip and the bamboo made a sharp rapping sound that added a mental component to the physical sting. She had no time to focus on it, though, because her foe's weapon had already been withdrawn and whipped toward her again, now at head height.

She dropped into a crouch, spun the jo staff, and brought it up behind the swinging sword as it passed over her. With her weapon, she guided it past and stepped forward to lunge a front kick at Sensei Ikehara's exposed ribs. He skittered away and released the sword to free his near hand. Before she could act on her momentary advantage, he simultaneously caught the weapon with the other hand and caught her ankle to give it a subtle twist.

The only thing she could do was to throw herself into a roll to avoid having the joint broken, and by the time she regained her bearings, the sword tip was at the back of her neck. Her teacher's voice was amused. "Do you yield?"

"Yes, Sensei." She sighed. "You've defeated me yet again."

He laughed as she turned to face him. "It may not feel like it, but you are improving. Your speed, your balance, and your comfort with the staff are all greater than they were only a month ago." His white uniform was pristine, as always, and he'd moved from close-cropped hair to a shaven head recently, which she thought was a good look for the man. His usually professionally serious face was transformed when he laughed, and it was always a delight to see it, even when she was frustrated.

His genuine praise in the face of her failure mollified her a little and she shook her head and lowered herself to sit cross-legged. She waited until her teacher had mirrored her to reply. "I get that. But things around me are accelerating faster than I'm improving. That'll eventually create a real problem, you know?"

He nodded. "But it's only possible to do so much unless you have magic to change the flow of time." With a grin, he asked, "You don't, do you?"

Cali chuckled and tried to keep her worry from showing. "No, unfortunately. As far as I know, that's not a power anyone has."

"Well, then, all you can do is your best. If you can't devote more hours to training, is there a way to slow the events around you?"

"Some yes, some no. I have a couple of weeks, at least, until the local troublemakers make their next attempt. And it's possible to delay the next fight with those in New Atlantis for a while. But those are small things and the rest are really big."

She hadn't often seen her teacher look hesitant, but that

was the only way to interpret his expression. "Have you considered my offer to fight at your side?"

Cali nodded. "I would welcome it, but not until I can find a weapon that would provide you with an effective countermeasure to the magical powers you might face. I asked Zeb and my sticks can't be used by anyone else without a fair amount of spell work I don't know how to do, so that's out."

"That makes sense. I regret that I can't help more now, though."

"I would have been killed countless times over if not for your teachings. You've done more than I could have expected or asked for."

"Still."

"I appreciate it, Sensei." She arched her back and stretched, then looked at the high ceiling. "Have you taken precautions?"

"I have." He sounded angry. She knew it wasn't directed at her but rather at those who would force innocent bystanders into a conflict. He'd been irate when she'd explained what the Atlantean gang had done. "I am always armed, and my family remains extra aware of their surroundings. But I'm sure the resolution you forced will stand."

She released the stretch. "I agree, it should and it probably will. But they've shown a willingness to color outside the lines before and I don't want to assume anything."

"In most cultures, attacking a family member is a transgression worthy of war."

Her spread hands and hunched shoulders betrayed her frustration and helplessness. "I've asked around about that.

Apparently, I could declare a blood feud if I had incontrovertible evidence of who did it. But since I didn't personally catch them in the act, it would be considered second-hand and thus not definitive. Or something. I think they must have a special caste of lawyers trying to make the rules difficult down there."

He laughed. "Well, perhaps you can find a way to put that to use as you learn more about how things work. Is it possible for you to bring allies from New Atlantis here to fight for you or take others there for those conflicts?

Cali frowned. "You know, I really should have thought of that. I considered it in terms of going down there but not the other way around. I wonder if there are schisms enough that I could find someone who might have a beef with the Atlantean gang here. That would be a real surprise for them when we battle again."

Ikehara inclined his head. "So, that's one problem with a path forward. Perhaps two if you can find people down there willing to fight with you in both places. Now, the next challenge is locating the pieces of the sword, is that correct?"

She nodded. "Even the ones we know about—well, we're only sure of one, really, and that is temporarily beyond our reach."

"Perhaps it's enough to be aware of its location for now. What's stopping you from seeking the others?"

"Finding them, basically. I hope my parents' codebook has some clues, but there's no guarantee it will. Emalia plans to work on it when we get to New Atlantis."

He stood and moved to replace his sword on the wall where it was usually mounted.

"Well, then, Cali, it sounds like all roads lead under the sea for you right now."

"Indeed, Sensei." She laughed and rose.

His smile was encouraging. "Prepare for class. You will all work extra hard today."

It had been an easy night at the Tavern, which was good since her body screamed from the workout Ikehara had put his students through that morning. She'd spent a total of at least an hour between then and work under the hot spray of her shower across several sessions but was still sore. It seemed there were muscles she didn't use very often and her teacher had exploited every one of them during the group session.

Something struck her arm and she flinched and almost dropped the tray filled with empty glasses. It turned out to be a gesticulating wizard who'd smacked her with his wand, but her nerves were no less jangled at the discovery. She made her way carefully to the front and set the tray down, then took a seat across from her boss.

He shook his head. "You're going too hard, Cali." Fyre snorted agreement from his position at the back of the bar but sent her only good feelings over their mental connection.

She shrugged and accepted the glass of cider he put before her. "I don't see another option, do you? Other than hiding in the basement with my hands over my ears and my eyes closed, that is."

The dwarf gave a short laugh. "Well, there's some truth

to that. You could probably hide in New Atlantis. Lie low and avoid the people trying to kill you."

Cali shook her head. "That doesn't protect any of you from them, though. It merely removes me and I'm safe for the next couple of weeks, anyway."

"Why are you so jumpy, then?"

To delay her answer, she sipped her cider, but he refused to release the hard stare he had fixed on her. With a sigh, she lowered the glass to the bar. "I'm doing a terrible job of keeping it all out of my head, I guess."

He nodded. "Then you definitely need to hit the road. Break the associations that trigger the bad thoughts and find a little peace, even if it's momentary."

"You wouldn't know what to do without me."

The dwarf laughed. "Don't worry. Janice is available."

Cali's retort was lost in the sound of Tanyith's bellow, "A drink, barkeep, before I die of thirst." She twisted to look at the door, where he stood with a silly grin, apparently in a buoyant mood.

He slid into the seat beside her. "What's up, sour-face?"

She raised an eyebrow and looked across the bar. "I'm sure he's talking to you, Zeb."

Her boss pointed at his lips, which were turned up in a smile. "And I'm sure not."

"Shut up, you. Both of you." She sighed and swiveled to face the new arrival. "What's your deal? Is someone having a sale on hair gel that got you all worked up?"

He grinned and stroked his high pompadour. With the shaved sides beneath, it really was a decent look for him. "While I appreciate you noticing my good looks—seriously, how could you not—no, that's not it. I have a lead."

"On your mystery man?"

"Dray came up with something out of nowhere. I guess he felt like he owed me one, even though I didn't join his gang. I plan to do a little recon this evening."

Cali glanced at Zeb, who gave her a slight nod. "I can leave early to give you a hand."

Tanyith shook his head. "Nah, tonight should be easy. If it needs more than me, I'll text you and wait till you're done. You gotta pay the rent, right?"

She laughed. "Right. And I'd better get back to that." Although the monthly payment she received from the trust her parents had put in place for her was a dependable income source, it wasn't sufficient to meet all her needs. Working was still required.

Plus, I'm not really cut out for a life of leisure, even if I am allegedly noble. A fast-moving bench scraped behind her and she turned with a sigh to intervene in whatever argument was about to break out.

CHAPTER FIFTEEN

D ray's tip had brought Tanyith to a location he'd never expected to see again. While the Shark Nightclub was the Atlantean gang's main hangout, a number of them had spent many nights at another one, far enough away from the headquarters that they could be reasonably assured of privacy. He hadn't visited since his return from Trevilsom and lacked the desire to go down the rabbit hole of his motivations around that.

Let's call it a lack of time. Yeah.

The Otter was a strange little bar located on the third floor of a corner building above a drugstore at street level and a voodoo shop on the second. The narrow staircase forced incoming patrons to halt at a lower floor to allow those exiting to get past. More than one fight had happened in that cramped space and the poorly patched walls provided a historical record of sorts. He smiled at the sight of a familiar scar, the result of his actions on a particularly revel-filled evening.

But a bad memory balanced every good one, with the

latter clustered toward the time immediately before he'd been sent away—suspicion, frustration, and arguments over whether to stay with the gang or break off and form another. To be back was bittersweet, at best.

The large single room that comprised the venue looked exactly as he remembered it. The stairs entered at the rear of one of the longer walls and the bar sat directly in front of it along a short one. Windows and booths covered the other two sides of the rectangle, with high-top tables between. No servers worked at the Otter, and the only food was prepackaged bags of chips and snacks, bought with your drink from the bartenders.

He walked to stand at the bar in his usual place, the far side that gave him a view of the entry door. It put his back to a window, but he'd always assumed that if a sniper targeted him, he'd be toast anyway. The bar had no seats, only a footrail and room to lean. The bartender hadn't changed either. He claimed his name was Otto, although no one believed it. He did have the stocky build and thick black mustache to support his claim of German origin, at least around those who only knew that country from cartoons and television shows. His bald head had sweat on it as he bustled from customer to customer.

In moments, Tanyith had Rye on the rocks in front of him as if no time had passed since his last visit. He nodded and slid a twenty across, which would get him a couple more. For the regulars, which he had been, the bar operated more by instinct than by numbers. When Otto felt you were paid up, drinks came without hesitation. When they slowed, you forked over more money or went home.

The lack of other familiar faces was the only reason

why it didn't feel like a place he belonged. He didn't recognize the second bartender, nor any of the patrons in the mostly filled booths, the couples at the high-tops, and the other hard-looking people who stood closest to where the alcohol lived. But he was early and the man Dray told him to look for hadn't ever been one to arrive until late.

Tanyith knew that well since Karam had been his best friend and mentor before he'd been ripped from his life and sent to Trevilsom. He'd looked for him after his return to the city but hadn't found a single clue until Dray connected the man to Aiden Walsh and told him where and when he might be found. He leaned on the bar, filled with equal parts anticipation and fear. In truth, it would be easiest if the man was mistaken so he could go back to his fruitless search with his past image of Karam untouched.

The next person to enter banished that fantasy. The man's look, the manner in which he walked, and the wry smile that always seemed to grace his face immediately told Tanyith that nothing had changed. It might have been twenty-four months before at the start of another night of carousing and arguing over the differences between what was right, what was practical, and what was good. He tensed at the sight of the older man, ready to pursue him if it became necessary. But the way the new arrival's face blossomed into a grin dispelled all his fears.

Karam was big and burly, equal parts muscle and flesh, and almost six and a quarter foot tall with brown hair in dreadlocks that hung to his waist. His skin was dark, pitted here and there with the signs of an acne-filled young adulthood, and his button-down shirt looked expensive, as did the khakis below and the shining boots visible under them.

He wrapped Tanyith in a hug and when they separated, he discovered he still remembered the ritual hand slaps the gang members had practiced in their subgroup.

His voice was low, pitched to not carry, as always. "Shale, when did you get back?"

Tanyith shook his head. "A while ago. I looked for you. Where have you been hiding?"

The other man shrugged and took the shot the bartender handed him. He downed it and followed it with a long pull on the beer that accompanied it. "Around. Here and there. You're not thinking about rejoining, are you?"

"Oh, hell no. That wench wound up in charge exactly like we thought she would."

He nodded. "I left shortly after you vanished. No one would give me any real answers, but I did have the sense that people knew and wouldn't talk. I couldn't be a part of that crew anymore because of it. I was sure they'd killed you. It took six months before someone finally told me where you'd disappeared to, and I assumed you were a goner. How did you get back?"

His laugh sounded a little brittle. "Explaining that would take days. Suffice it to say that another group of scumbags decided I could be of use to them and broke me out to set their hook deep."

"Ouch." He slid a bill across the bar and new drinks appeared for them both moments later. "So, something tells me it might not be only luck that puts us both here at the same time, hey?"

Tanyith nodded and lowered his voice even more. "Dray mentioned you sometimes hung out here. I helped him with an issue a while back, and I guess he thought the scales were still unbalanced. He directed me to you to put them right."

"And you wanted to find me because?" He sounded cautious but not suspicious.

"I missed you?" After a brief pause, they both laughed. *It feels almost like old times. I'd forgotten in all the bad that there was so much good, too.* He shook his head. "I'm looking for someone for a friend. Well, hell, for Sienna. You remember her."

He grinned. "How could I not? You were stupid for her."

"And continue to be, apparently. Anyway, she misplaced her ex-boyfriend and wants to find him. She still carries a flame or something."

Karam's face turned sour. "So, let me get this right. You —who might or might not have a thing for Sienna—said you'd try to find her ex-boyfriend and you're actually doing it?" He finished the beer in his glass. "You're the same idiot I remember, Tay."

They laughed again with the easy camaraderie forged over time. "Yeah, I guess I am, at that. So, how about you catch me up with everything you know about the old gang, starting with Aiden Walsh?"

His friend's lips turned down at the mention of the name and he collected the full glasses that had appeared and carried them to a booth in the corner. Tanyith slid in across from him, and his old friend shook his head. "Okay, so let's start with the man of the hour. Aiden went underground. I hear he pops up now and again but is generally absent—like he's out of town or something but comes through on business on the regular."

Tanyith frowned. "Well, damn. That'll make intercepting him difficult. Do you have any names of people who might know when he'll be around?"

Karam shook his head. "I really don't. But I'll spread the word and see what I can find."

"Do it quietly. From what I've been able to put together, he's become a serious piece of bad news since Sienna knew him. I always thought he was a jerk but not a player."

"Based on what I hear, you missed that call."

He nodded. "It seems like it. So, who else?"

His companion listed a number of names, all of which were vaguely familiar but none of which summoned a face to his mind. "They're all working together—kind of a merry band of idiots—doing petty crimes. Their team hits stores at night, that kinda garbage."

The man's words jogged a memory. "Hey, wait—they weren't behind the robbery at Maurier's place, were they?"

Karam nodded. "Yep, far as I know. Why do you ask?"

"Bennie's a friend of mine from way back through Sienna. More importantly, he has a family and a kid who's going through medical issues. He would have been on the don't touch list in our day." They had always been careful to research the people they targeted and stuck mostly to those who could afford a little loss. When they screwed up, which they did sometimes, they made good in an anonymous way.

His old friend snorted. "There aren't enough brains among them to make a list, much less follow it. They're all about targets of opportunity. I doubt they even have a plan, merely smash, grab, and run."

"Still. It doesn't give them the right to take from those without enough to spare."

The man shrugged. "No one cares. They're too small for the police to worry about in any serious way, and the gangs that used to look out for folks are busy feuding with each other."

Or with others, but point taken. Tanyith frowned. "So, how about this? You work on finding more information for me on Aiden Walsh and we'll meet here for a longer night of catching up when my schedule eases in a week or so. I have a friend who needs help between now and then."

Karam nodded. "That sounds good. It's awful nice to see you back, Tay."

"And you, Ram." He stood to leave, then snapped his fingers as if a thought had occurred to him. "You don't know where those boys who hit Bennie's place hole up, do you?"

He shook his head. "Nah. You're not asking for any particular reason, are you?"

"I thought I might look 'em up."

"Well, if you decide that you want to do something about it, feel free to reach out. I wouldn't mind taking a stroll down memory lane and kicking some asses that desperately need it."

"You got it, brother." *And I know exactly who to ask to get a lead on where they are.*

CHAPTER SIXTEEN

Kendra Barton was out and about when he called, so they agreed to meet at a small restaurant that stayed open all night to give the workers closing the bars somewhere to unwind before they wandered home for much-needed sleep. She was already there when he arrived, tucked in a booth with a cup of coffee and a Coke in front of her. Her short black hair drooped into her eyes, and she wore a black top under her heavy black leather jacket. He slid in across from her and stole a sip. "Cherry. The best of the flavors."

She scowled at him. "You know, a booty call at one am is something I might have expected and even welcomed. But calling when I'm out having a few drinks so I can work for you is cold, Tay. Damn cold." The words came out with a smile, but he heard the truth behind them too. He'd been busy, but he'd also kept his distance a little. What she'd said about him straddling the line rather than choosing a side hadn't sat well with him.

"No rest for the wicked, so they say. But I think you'll

be glad you decided to answer when you hear what I need."

After a moment, she nodded. "All right. Lay it on me."

He had to wait while the server slid the plate with her burger and fries in front of her. She gestured for him to start while she ate. "Okay, so, I ran into an old friend tonight—a good one. He told me it's members of our former club who have pulled a number of the smaller hit-and-run robberies around town."

His companion frowned as she chewed, swallowed, and followed it with a gulp of coffee. "It's not really my area unless you're telling me it's on behalf of one of the gangs."

"Nah, they are strictly small fish. But they're indiscriminate and it's only a matter of time before the idiots do something bigger like shoot someone while they're stoned and looking to steal munchies."

Kendra snorted and coughed around the food in her mouth. When she could speak again, she pointed a French fry at him. "That's attempted murder right there. You did that on purpose."

"Nope." He shook his head. "It was totally random, Detective. So, are you able to hack the system or whatever it is you do and check to see if there's any info on them?"

She rolled her eyes. "Yes. I can search the database. You weren't gone long enough to be this much of a Luddite. Read a book, Shale." She dug into the pocket of her leather jacket, retrieved her heavy-duty cop phone, and ran through the security protections he found decidedly over-done. Finally, she typed a few things and swiped the screen. After a couple of minutes—during which he snatched fries from her plate when she wasn't looking—she raised her gaze to focus on him.

"Okay, these people are scumbags, you're right. They robbed a damn church. Who does that?"

"My guess is it's more stupidity than evilness—drunk or high and simply taking whatever target presents itself. Although maybe I'm wrong and they're a super-secret criminal organization trying to appear to be idiots to throw suspicion off. What I need is a location. Do you have anything?"

Barton frowned in concentration. "Okay, that's a little extra challenging. Fortunately, these babies have more computing power than you'd think." She typed quickly into the device and he stole a sip of her drink. Without looking up, she growled annoyance. "Order your own, freeloader."

He laughed and walked to the counter to do so. When he returned, she slid the phone across to him. "I put in a search for all the petty theft above the level of street grabs and asked the system to plot them on a map. It's a very interesting result if you ask me."

It took him several seconds to understand what he was looking at, but the pattern soon became clear. The incidents formed a rough semi-circle, and more or less at the midpoint of that was one of the abandoned industrial areas that lay on the fringes of the touristy parts of the city near the docks. "So, your computers think this is where they're based?"

Kendra nodded. "That'd be my guess." His food arrived and she chewed a fry thoughtfully while he poured ketchup on his burger. "The question is, what do you plan to do about it?"

Tanyith met her gaze. "Do you suggest I should report it

to the police? The same police who haven't seen fit to address it because they have bigger things to deal with?"

She shook her head. "No. I know you won't do that. And you're right, it wouldn't get any attention. But you can't simply turn into a serial killer."

He winced at the reference to Cali's parents, who the detective believed were vigilantes and had committed serious crimes, although he didn't share her conviction. *There's more to that story, I'm sure of it.* He shrugged. "I don't need to kill anyone to take back what they stole as long as I'm careful about it. Hell, if I'm good enough, I can probably accomplish it without any hubbub at all."

Her laughter was a welcome sound. "Hubbub. Sometimes, you seem like someone transported here from a century ago, you know that?"

"If so, I'm holding up well for my age." He grinned in mock challenge.

Kendra raised an eyebrow. "I'd have to see more to be sure. Maybe after you're done with whatever it is you plan to do you should give me a call."

"I'll do that. Count on it."

Tanyith considered calling Karam in to assist but felt a reluctance he decided not to override.

It's been a long time, and people change. Perhaps we need a little more opportunity to get to know each other again before we engage in criminal activities together.

His first stop was Cali's bunker. He had her permission to be there whenever he felt the need but it continued to strike him as weird any time he was alone there. *Like I'm treading on hallowed ground that doesn't want me here.* They'd examined the structure with every magic they could and had found nothing that would instill that feeling. Still, there it was.

He crossed to the locker that had been Thomas Leblanc's and removed the black uniform. Once he'd stripped his street clothes off and donned the outfit, he located and affixed the patches to cover the house sigil. He'd decided to leave his Sai at home as they were rare enough to be a clue to his identity.

Magic and whatever I can find there should be more than enough. The reinforced uniform will give me all the edge I need to deal with these losers.

To do any preparation at all was mainly a hedge against there being more trouble than he expected to encounter in their home base. If the indications Kendra had found were true, the petty criminals wouldn't be able to stand up against someone with his skill set. Still, it never hurt to be over-prepared. He pulled the reinforced boots on, laced them tightly, and made sure the pouch containing his thief's tools was in place. As he took one last look around the room, a thought struck him.

It's weird that there are no weapons here. Maybe her parents were really good at magic and didn't need any, but you'd think they would have had some as a backup plan, at least.

With a shrug, he dismissed it as a question for a different day.

His nearest portal location to the target area was in an alley close to the docks, and he stepped through first to his apartment and then to the place near the river. Keeping the existence of the bunker a secret was an overriding priority, more sacred than preventing a bystander from seeing his home through the magical rip in space. A cargo ship was being unloaded nearby, and the shouts of the workers and the creak and hum of machinery echoed all around. He pulled up the map function on his phone and headed toward the location he'd marked.

The constant need to look up and down to track his progress soon became irritating. *What I need is a pair of those augmented reality goggles, like they use in the Army.* He snorted. *Sure, I'll break into a military base and get some. Easy-peasy. Kendra would love that.*

Tanyith remained on the shortest route to his destination nonetheless and within minutes, reached the fringe of a small town of seemingly abandoned industrial buildings. A grid of streets separated them, as perfectly uniform as the structures themselves. The only variation was in the names and logos of those who'd been the last to occupy them.

He took care to hug the structures and remain in the shadows thrown by the overpowered streetlights above. Only one in three still functioned, but that was enough to betray him if he wasn't careful. It was also enough to discern a thin trail of smoke that emanated from the corner of a rooftop. He shook his head. They really were amateurs.

At the next street, he moved right to gain distance from the apparent lookout, followed by a left turn to position himself under the darkest place he could see at the next building. He launched himself with force magic and landed four stories above in a quiet crouch.

Careful to remain as quiet as possible, he crept across the cool black surface until he was opposite the smoker's position. It was no longer visible, which meant either that the sentry had moved or had finished whatever he'd been smoking. He used the next fifteen minutes to watch quietly for any evidence of a presence from the other building.

Maybe it wasn't a lookout at all but someone who snuck up for a drag. In any case, it's a sign that there are people inside and they're not very smart.

Tanyith had taken note of a small structure that covered the stairs in the middle of the roof he was on as he crossed it and knew there would be a similar feature on the one his quarry had selected. He hurtled over the street, landed in a skid on the target building, and spun as he landed to face the position where the smoke had come from. His boots slipped on the tiny rocks at his feet but he regained his balance without mishap. The rooftop was clear.

If it had been his stronghold, he would have put cameras or alarms or something in place on all accesses. Even though he guessed this group didn't possess a particularly strategic mindset, it would be foolish to assume they wouldn't have taken at least some similar precautions.

I have to move fast but quietly. He found the entrance to the staircase unlocked and opened it as he shook his head. *If this really is the group Karam thinks it is, they're dumber than I remember.*

He descended with care and paused at the door at the bottom, which was locked. His power lockpick made quick work of the barrier, and he returned it to the belt pouch at the small of his back.

All right, chuckleheads, let's see what you're hiding.

CHAPTER SEVENTEEN

The door opened toward him, and he eased it only enough to peer out. It led to a larger stairwell with triple-wide steps, metal railings and protective gates, and concrete surfaces that were likely to echo. He traversed this with extra caution and managed to keep the sound of his intrusion to a minimum. Another door stood at the end. Tanyith pressed his ear to it but heard nothing of significance. He pulled slowly to open it inch by inch so he could explore what lay beyond.

The company that had once occupied it had apparently bought into the open-office plan. A central block of beige cubicle walls with the only visible walk space on the perimeter greeted him. He stuck his head out to look in the opposite direction and discovered more of the same. To be sure, he stepped through and wandered the entire floor but found no one.

He descended cautiously to the next level and pressed his ear to the door again. This time, he heard voices beyond, crouched, and drew it open only far enough to risk a look. On this floor, the cubicles had been dismantled and pushed to the far end and a group of four men sat around two L-shaped desks shoved together to create a large table. They held cards carefully away from the others' eyes, and poker chips and bottles of beer littered the surface. Cigarettes were stuck between at least two pairs of lips, so whatever the person on the roof had indulged in, it probably hadn't been tobacco. The nearest man wore a belt holster on his hip and a pistol butt protruded from it.

Tanyith took a second to consider his quandary. He'd hoped to infiltrate quietly, find the storage area, and sneak out with the most valuable and portable pieces they'd stolen but not yet sold. That would have been the easiest option and also carried the least risk. To continue with that plan would mean leaving enemies at his tail—which seemed like a bad notion, strategically speaking.

Especially since at least one of them is armed. He shook his head. While the smart move would be to leave and return another day, his desire to teach them a lesson grew with each stupid word that left their mouths as they played. *No, they deserve to get what's coming to them. I'm the lucky one who is the delivery vehicle.*

His mind made up, he settled in to wait and assumed that at some point, one or more of the men would need to take a break. Sure enough, not too much later, the first man walked toward the back of the space where a restroom sign was affixed to the wall. Tanyith cast a veil to hide himself and followed him in. It was a simple matter to get behind him and apply a chokehold to render him unconscious. As he lowered the thug gently to the floor, he congratulated himself on a strong start. His good feelings about it lasted only a moment before the door opened to reveal another of the card players.

He cursed inwardly as the cigarette fell from the man's lips and his hand fumbled for his weapon. His instinctive force bolt hurled his opponent out of the doorway and across the main room. He raced out and angled toward the others, sure that it would take the jerk a few moments to recover.

Assuming I didn't kill him. That was a little harder than intended. The first to get his pistol free had it knocked out of his grip with another force bolt, and he did the same with the remaining card player's gun a moment later. Their shouts were unfortunate but probably wouldn't carry as far as a gunshot would have.

Before they could react, he drove his booted heel into the closer adversary's knee and the surprised man collapsed with a wail. The second managed to draw a butterfly knife and stab at him with it, but the reinforced forearm in the uniform stopped the blade as he blocked it and pushed it upward to expose the man's ribs. They snapped beneath his sidekick and the injury dropped the thug to his knees.

Tanyith spun to check on the enemy he'd blasted across the room, who was out cold but fortunately still breathing. He focused on controlling his own breath as he circled the room to collect weapons and cell phones. Phone cords proved useful as a substitute for rope, and he bound two men to one another and the others to nearby hardpoints.

With that finished, he stashed the guns and phones in a trash bin and headed down to the second floor. A single glance through the slightly open door revealed the items he'd hoped to find. The cubicles had been cleared but the desks remained, each of them stacked with stolen goods of one type or another, plus a couple covered with weapons. The one to the farthest left supported a money counter, bound bills, and velvet bags that doubtless contained jewels or other expensive items.

A single man stood guard in the room, positioned at the far window through which he gazed out at the brighter lights of the main part of the city. An assault rifle was slung casually over his shoulder.

Damn. Maybe these jerks aren't as amateur as I assumed if they pack that kind of heat.

All his primary options for removing the man from this distance would probably also hurl him through the glass in front of him, so he crept through the doorway and eased it closed. An open lane ran down to his right, and he transited it without detection. He turned left at the end with the intention to move beside the windows so he could blast his target parallel to them. The desks blocked his way and he muttered imprecations under his breath. The part of his mind that told him to go loud and not worry about the window pushed obstinately against the more rational portion. He gritted his teeth, cast a veil in front of him, and climbed over the obstacles.

Two things were immediately apparent when he reached the top of the final piece of furniture. First, the man was clearly a magical—as many or all of the group's members doubtless were, even if they chose to carry guns. He turned at the appearance of the cloaking spell as if he'd somehow sensed the magic. Second, removing the desks from their support walls had apparently compromised their fundamental stability. The surface under his feet wobbled, and he hurled himself forward in a diving roll as the guard twisted to raise his gun into a firing position.

Tanyith barely managed to summon a force shield in time to catch the barrage of bullets that erupted from the weapon. Magical or not, the man's aim proved to be excellent and he delivered tightly grouped rounds that forced him to maintain precise concentration so his defense wouldn't falter. His foe backed away slowly, and a quick glance at the door betrayed his intentions.

Oh no you don't. He extended his protective barrier to full height as he stood and raced toward the man.

The guard seemed momentarily surprised when his magazine ran out of bullets but recovered quickly to launch a shadow magic blast. Tanyith shifted the nature of the shield to better match the incoming attack but doing so slowed him. The small grin on his opponent's face as he neared the door inspired a snarl, and he released the power he'd been building. The two desks closest to his enemy careened at the man like they'd been kicked. He yelped and managed to conjure a hasty shield, but it wasn't sufficient to absorb the full momentum of the projectiles. The metal furniture formed a sandwich with the wall and crushed him inside.

So much for subtlety. Between the gunfire and the crashing equipment, the time for sneaking had definitely reached an end. However, two possible options now confronted him. The first was an extreme desire to attack whoever no doubt raced to the stairs at that very moment. It surged through him and he took several steps in that direction before the other option found purchase in his brain. He hesitated, knowing the right choice wouldn't make him happiest but decided to follow it anyway.

Another wave of force magic lifted the other desks nearby and stacked them in front of the door to the staircase. The makeshift barricade wouldn't hold for long—seconds at the most—but it would probably be all he needed.

He sprinted to the desk at the far end and snatched up a random sack from one of the others on the way. Impatient, he emptied it of the stuffed animals it held—*Seriously, you guys, what the hell are you thinking?*—and shoved bills and velvet bags into it. He turned to look for more but the sound of voices and footsteps in the stairwell stopped him.

With no time to waste, he jerked the bag closed, whirled toward the nearest window, and pushed into a sprint. As he approached, he raised a hand to shatter the glass with a force bolt and the shards exploded into the night. He followed a moment later and used a force blast to boost him up and over onto the next roof.

Tanyith looked back as the piled desks catapulted away from the door. He raced to the far edge, jumped, and again, force magic cushioned his landing. Once out of their sight, he conjured a portal and stepped through it to safety.

The church was one of the oldest in New Orleans, an Episcopalian ministry that had extended open arms to the magical community as well. In his time with the Atlantean gang several years before, it had provided a no-questions-asked refuge for anyone and everyone who needed it. The only rule had been that all involved observed the rules of sanctuary. High-level meetings among enemies who would have felt comfortable meeting nowhere else had taken place during the late-night hours on a number of occasions. He imagined the main congregation would no doubt have supported that service had they been aware of it.

A woman who had spent her childhood on the streets had been the priest of the church for almost a decade. He recalled her powerful and animated preaching style, but her most memorable feature was her determination to ensure that what was right was accomplished, regardless of anything that might get in the way. She would be the perfect person for this job.

Her home stood on the church grounds, a small single-family dwelling. He searched carefully and saw no evidence of a security system, although he wasn't at all surprised. It was known on the streets that anyone who targeted her would find themselves declared persona non grata and hunted by all sides, which possibly made her the safest person in the city. Whether she knew it or not, he had no idea, but she doubtless trusted in her deity to keep her safe if that was his or her will. In any case, it made tonight's work easier.

He had stopped and bundled the items he'd taken from the not-so-petty thieves into a box and included a note. It instructed her to make sure Bennie received a portion and shared his suspicions about where the loot had come from. He trusted her judgment from there, whether to direct it to those who had lost it or to distribute it to those in greater need. Aside from the fact that he didn't have time to worry about the distribution, he readily acknowledged that it simply wasn't his forte.

No, Anastasia will do a much better job than I ever would. He picked the lock, slid the container inside, then quietly reset the lock and closed the door.

With that successfully accomplished, he walked to a position where he wouldn't be noticed and called in an anonymous tip on the group's location. That might result in a little more of the stolen property finding its way home.

Finally, he punched Kendra's number in and a wide smile spread across his face as she picked up after a single ring and demanded, "Why aren't you here yet?"

CHAPTER EIGHTEEN

Cali's night hadn't turned out the way she'd expected. When Tanyith had declined her offer to assist him in whatever adventure he had undertaken, she'd had visions of normal things ahead—sleep, maybe an enjoyable meal beforehand, and possibly even catching up on some of the homework she somehow routinely neglected. Instead, there she was in the very early morning hours, watching the front door of the Shark Nightclub. Fyre sat on the rooftop beside her, his eyes also locked on the entrance.

"Are you sure about what you heard?" she asked again,

The Draksa sounded exasperated, possibly because he'd answered the same question a number of times already. "Yes, I'm positive of it."

"You were flying fast and fighting. You could be mistaken." Part of her had doubts but the rest simply enjoyed messing with him. Fortunately, in this circumstance, she could indulge both.

He stared at her, unblinking, for almost half a minute

before he answered. "I heard what I heard. There will be a special delivery of some kind tonight at the club."

She shook her head. "They could be portaling in."

"They could." He nodded.

"It could be a trap."

"It could."

"We should probably leave."

His snort almost made her laugh but she stopped it in time. "Please. You're physically and mentally incapable of letting something like this go and you know it."

"You're not wrong." She sighed.

A sound from below drew their attention to a car that pulled up to the curb in front of the nightspot. A man in the standard gang uniform emerged, carrying a large cylinder like architects sometimes used to transport blue-prints. The way he held it made it seem as if it weighed a fair amount.

Cali breathed deeply. "Okay. Here goes." She calcu-lated the angles and raised her hand, the palm facing the sky. On it was one of the gadgets from the bunker, which Emalia had found a description of in the coded book. It was a magical marker, and she'd be able to track it since she'd familiarized herself with its signature. She used a flick of force magic to send it in a long arc toward the target and grinned in satisfaction when it struck and stuck to the cylinder, too small to be easily noticed.

"Nice shot." Fyre commented.

She shrugged. "Yeah, I'm thinking of going pro next year. I definitely have what it takes." She turned and sat with her back against the low wall that ran around the top edge of the building. "Now, we wait. Then, when they're all gone, we break in and take it."

It was several hours before the man exited as part of the wave of people leaving the Nightclub. There was good news and bad news. The good was that the person accompanying him locked the front door, which suggested that he was the last to leave. The bad was that even though she couldn't see the cylinder, the magical tracker told her he still had. "Damn it. He didn't drop it off."

"Or he exchanged what was inside for something else. Or it's empty."

Cali considered it but none of the options seemed to make sense. *Okay, fifty-fifty chance. Do I think it's more likely that they'd keep valuables in the club, or not?* "I think they're playing us. They've set a trap inside but the actual item is still in the container."

Fyre tilted his head to the side for a moment in thought before he nodded. "I agree."

"Okay. Let's follow that car."

The Draksa took to the air while she used the rooftops where she could and only descended to street level when the jumps were too far. They trailed the vehicle to a storage building—one of the type that had become popular and contained garages or closets for rent. Thankfully, they were able to find a good vantage point on a rooftop across from it. The car pulled inside one at ground level, and a few moments later, the men emerged, pulled the door down, and locked it with a heavy padlock.

"So. Whatever he brought is in there."

"Probably hidden. Probably under lock and key. Probably in a giant safe guarded by an octopus." Her companion obviously couldn't help himself and an odd sound might have been a suppressed laugh confirmed her suspicions. He'd deliberately built up to the octopus finale.

She shook her head. "I can't imagine there's that kind of security in there. Unless they've portaled it out—which doesn't make sense—we should be able to get to it."

The Draksa snorted. "There could be a horde of them waiting to try to kill you."

Cali shrugged. "That would be a bonus."

He rolled his eyes. "So, you're determined, then?"

"You know it."

A shimmer in the air around him signaled the activation of his veil. "All right, then. Let's do it."

He led the way to ground level, froze the lock, and broke it with a swipe of his claw. She darted out of the shadows and rolled under the door, which he lifted barely enough for her to get under. While he remained outside as a guard, she called a fireball up and floated it to provide illumination, fully prepared for an ambush.

The garage-like space contained only a car—a piece of junk from the late eighties, by the looks of it, that was somehow still running. She popped the trunk with the lever inside the cab and located the cylinder. Cautiously, she tested it with her magic but it revealed nothing sinister or defensive. A long, thin, black box was tucked within and she opened it carefully to find a piece of a blade covered in familiar etchings. A card inside read, *The perfect bait,* and was signed only *SM.*

"Take off. I'll portal home from here," She sent to Fyre, He returned assent and she opened a gate to an alley on Bourbon Street with her magic. She wasn't sure what she'd found, but was positive that she'd done the right thing by not following it into the club. When she reached her destination, she ditched everything but the metal shard in a dumpster and opened another portal, this one to her parents' bunker.

It's Time to gather all the pieces and take them somewhere useful.

CHAPTER NINETEEN

Emalia had packed several cases to take with her to New Atlantis, and she levitated them through the portal while Cali watched. Once again, she was jealous of the older woman's easy access to telekinesis, which was one of the magics that continued to elude her. She tried now and again in private but rarely managed to make things move in the way she wanted them to. The closest she'd come was when she managed to tip a vase she'd really liked, which of course rolled off the table and shattered on the floor.

Her great aunt turned to her with a smile. "Well, that's all the luggage. I think we're ready to depart."

At her side, Fyre leaned into Cali and said, "Let's go. Move it. Time's a-wasting."

She scowled at him. "What's your rush?"

He grinned and his tongue hung out of his mouth. "I can walk around in my natural form there, remember? Sometimes, being a dog is annoying. For one thing, people always try to find my owner when I'm alone. And don't get me started about the animal control guy." The Draksa rolled his eyes. "Anything that can run for more than twenty seconds at a time is safe from that dude."

"Gotcha." She laughed. "Fine. Go." She gestured and Fyre dashed through, followed by her great aunt at a more leisurely pace. After one last look around her, she stepped across the threshold and was immediately transported from the basement of the Drunken Dragons in New Orleans to the city of New Atlantis, far below the ocean's surface in the Bermuda Triangle. With a wave, she dismissed the magical rift and called, "Jenkins, we're home."

The disembodied voice of the Leblanc House's guardian spirit, for lack of a better word, answered immediately. "Welcome back, Matriarch. Hello, Fyre. And who have you brought with you if I might be so bold as to ask?"

The older woman smiled. "You may not recognize me, Jenkins, but we've met in the past. I'm Elisinia's aunt on her father's side."

His formal voice transformed and filled with warmth. "Miss Emalia! You've changed but you still sound exactly like yourself. It's so good to encounter you again."

She laughed. "And you as well."

Cali frowned. "You know, you might have warned me there was a ghost in the family mansion."

"What would have been the fun in that?" The other woman sounded carefree in a way she couldn't recall her being in the world above.

"How long is it since you've been here?"

She sighed. "It seems like a lifetime. Now, where will I stay?" Her luggage levitated in readiness.

"This way, Miss Emalia." Jenkins lit up the wall sconces on the correct path.

Cali shook her head but wasn't able to suppress her smile. "You two go ahead and catch up. Fyre and I have business to attend to. She has all the privileges of family, of course, Jenkins. Oh, and we'll have another guest later as well."

"Very good, Matriarch Caliste."

She looked at Fyre. "There is a surprise around every corner, appropriate for the cheap horror film my life has become."

He snorted. "Save the drama for a llama. Let's go for a walk."

"A llama?" She laughed as she pulled the front door open. "Where the hell did you learn that?"

Tanyith had arranged the meeting for that afternoon as a way to make them dance to her tune. They had more than enough time to reach the bar he'd described and stopped to place orders for food and drink to be delivered to the house. Jenkins had explained that while it was technically possible for him to oversee such things when it was fully staffed, it was far easier if she made the requests in person until she chose to return the Leblanc residence to its proper routines.

It had been very clear that restoring it meant she'd have to spend considerable time there, and while she really didn't mind the idea at all, it definitely wasn't the right moment for it. So she and Fyre selected fruits, vegetables, meats, ciders, and wines from appropriate shops. The Draksa knew more than she'd expected him to and sent waves of approval at her when she pointed at an item he preferred. The desire to keep his ability to speak secret was his, so she played along.

Her outfit attracted attention as she walked. She hadn't changed into anything New Atlantean as she preferred her shorts, sneakers, and t-shirt. As a matriarch, she'd follow the rules and fit in when it was required, but she would be herself for the rest of the time and to hell with anyone who didn't approve. Including the people she was about to visit, who could go to hell simply on general principles.

Cali had met a couple of the Malniets already and had fought one of them in a round of ritual combat. While she couldn't be sure, she imagined the others had been family but it was always possible they were only friends. In any case, she didn't expect to meet any of the people at the top of the food chain in this section of town. It made her wonder if the whole family was on the same page about their future.

It might be something we can exploit so it is worth keeping in mind.

When Tanyith had told her the name of the place, she'd laughed and he'd explained that his reaction had been exactly the same. But when she stepped inside the Privateer Pub, she discovered it wasn't nearly as bad as she'd expected. There was a bar to the left, seating areas in front and to her right, and a closed door separating a back area. He'd said that's where they'd be, so she turned and marched in that direction with Fyre at her heels.

The bartender yelled in a gruff voice, "Hey, no animals in here," but she ignored him and pushed through the door.

Beyond was a small room with a rectangular table, and a man sat behind it. What looked like pockmarks covered the parts of his face that weren't hidden by the goatee and oversized mustache. His heavy blue work shirt had a dark stain on the left arm that could easily have been blood. Fyre sent her a feeling of scorn and she had to agree. Apparently, he'd played the tough guy with Tay, but his demeanor struck her as weak.

"Matriarch Leblanc," he said in a rasping tone. "How lovely of you to visit."

She shook her head. "Stow it. Are you a Malniet?"

He nodded. "Not from the main line, of course. My people don't come from the big house."

"Pity. From what I've seen of them, you'd fit right in."

He grinned and revealed crooked teeth. "You have some sass, girl. Good. You'll need it for the noble-nine infighting. But that's neither here nor there. Do you have what we requested?"

Cali threw the cloth-wrapped package on the table. "Samples of both. But here's the thing. I'm not a big fan of you manipulating Tanyith. You might want to reconsider the threats you've made."

The man shrugged. "And you might want to reconsider the ones you're making. You have far more to lose here than I do. I can put your friend in prison again and vanish. You, on the other hand, will always have eyes on you—eyes that can be bought for the right price. No, you're in no position to issue demands, princess."

Fyre lurched forward with a growl and she extended a

hand to restrain him. "Now now. There's no point in killing him yet. I'm sure that we can come to an agreement."

The man looked a little pale but his nod was as disrespectful as his words had been. "There's already one in place, sweetie, and your boy has more to deliver. Tell him to watch for a message from us with his next task."

She shook her head. "You're treading on dangerous ground."

"As are you. Of the two of us, who do you think has more friends and who has more enemies?"

Unfortunately, she had no reply appropriate to the question so she turned and stalked out. She glared at the bartender when he seemed inclined to speak to her and slammed the door once she stepped through. "He's a jerk, but that doesn't make him wrong." Fyre nodded, and she shook her head. "This will be trickier than I thought." They walked into the late afternoon sun in companionable silence as she ran through possibilities in her mind.

When they arrived at the house, Cali opened a portal for Zeb. He looked over his shoulder once before he stepped through, doubtless worried about leaving the bar in Janice's hands.

Ha. Take that for all your teasing. I bet you wouldn't worry if it was me there. She located Emalia, and the three of them cooked a simple meal from the provisions that had been delivered.

They ate and laughed together while her boss and great

aunt told tales and tried to one-up each other. Fyre snorted occasionally from his position under the table, and even Jenkins joined in with a comment here and there, usually of disbelief at the most ridiculous points of the stories. She shook her head and washed the dishes while the other two departed to walk the house and examine the wards.

When the last plate was placed in the drying rack, she wiped her hands with a towel and hung it on its hook. "All right, buddy, how about we explore?"

The Draksa made a sound between a groan and a growl but a moment later, he was at her side. The part of the dwelling that remained unexplored was accessible only through a single entrance she'd completely missed in her wanderings. The door led into the space under the peaked roof and she would still be unaware of it if Jenkins hadn't asked her about it. He'd claimed not to have access but had recalled its existence seemingly at random. The spirit remained an enigma, but she chose to believe he had her best interests at heart—or at a minimum, her family's best interests. Currently, she saw no reason to doubt that those two things were in alignment.

Cali sent a thread of magic to the outline in the ceiling. It lowered slowly and trailed a ladder, which settled silently onto the floor. She looked into the darkness, then smiled at Fyre. "Do you want to take a look and let me know what you find?"

He barked a single growly laugh. "I do not. Your family, your risk."

"Traitor." They both knew it would be safe and it was simply a fun exchange of wordplay. She climbed only high enough to look into the room, ready to let herself fall if there was any danger. The darkness began to fade and soon, lanterns were visible at intervals, mounted on posts that connected the floor with the roof above. Seeing no threats, she ascended the rest of the way. "Come on up, coward."

The Draksa soared into the space with a swift flap of his wings and landed with his paws splayed around the entrance. He turned in a circle, then stepped to her side. "I sense no danger here."

"Me neither. Well, not physical danger, anyway." As the room reached full illumination, it was revealed as a workspace, much like a combination office and laboratory. It had a feel that reminded her of the bunker, and she knew intuitively that this was a place where her parents had spent considerable time together. "Emotional? Well, that's a different story." She shook her head and sighed. "Let's see what they left behind."

CHAPTER TWENTY

Wood was the dominant theme in the attic space as evidenced in the floor and the struts that reached up to the wooden braces that held the roof. Wooden chairs and desks all looked polished from long use. The darker wood of the apothecary cabinet, dressers, and wardrobe suggested they might be from a different era. A scent lingered in the air that seemed like vanilla sometimes and cinnamon at others.

She shook her head. "It fits them so well."

Fyre didn't respond but walked beside her as she approached the desks and sat behind the one on the right. Unlike in the office below, these were set side by side and butted up against each other. She pulled out the center drawer and found only a pad and pens. The drawers on the left held a variety of items, all of them boringly normal.

The other desk was the same. Neither held any revelations or something that might help her with any of her problems. Pushing down her frustration, Cali spun the chair, stood, and crossed to the wardrobe. She yanked it open, expecting it to be filled with uniforms or weapons, and discovered formal wear instead. The outfits were encased in transparent sheaths that weren't quite plastic and looked far more luxurious than what she'd found before.

She turned her head and asked the air, "Jenkins, are you up here now?"

A voice echoed from below. "No, Matriarch Caliste. I am still prevented from entering the space."

She chuckled. "Maybe you're a vampire spirit and need to be invited. I hereby allow you to access to this room."

He spoke from beside her. "Thank you, Miss Caliste. Ah, I see you have discovered your parents' official court garments."

"Explain." There were ten for her father and a matching number for her mother.

"Part of the role of matriarch and patriarch is to attend ceremonies at the palace and at the homes of the Nine or to host on occasion. Each outfit is appropriate for a gala at one of the noble houses or one held by the Empress. They contain elements that recognize the host and others that reflect the house of the wearer. It is quite complicated."

"Of course it is." She shook her head. "I bet I'll find matching jewelry in the cabinet, won't I?"

"That is a reasonable assumption."

She closed the wardrobe with a sigh and turned to the dresser. The apothecary cabinet with all its separate little square drawers enticed her, but she wanted to save it for dessert. Before she opened the top section, she played a mental guessing game.

Hmm. Maybe shoes or sweaters or something. Or underwear. Please don't let it be underwear.

It slid open with no problem to reveal an array of belts and straps separated into their own pockets by vertical panels. She lifted one from the right, which had been the side her mother's formalwear had been on. It looked about the correct size to go around her leg and had a loop on the inside. "So. That looks like a thigh sheath for a hidden weapon."

"Agreed, Matriarch Caliste."

She pawed through the remainder but failed to determine what any others were for. "Well, that's interesting. Let's try the next one." She slid it open and found hand-worked belts with the Leblanc seal emblazoned on them, both embossed into the leather and on a bright buckle. Small pouches of the same material with loops for the belt to pass through filled the rest of the space. "Nice."

"Those have been used by the matriarchs and patriarchs of House Leblanc for generations. I remember seeing them worn."

With a sigh, she slid the drawer closed without answering. The weight of inheriting the leadership of one of the Nine had suddenly trebled. *It's okay, Cali. You're up to this. Besides, there are no other options until you free Atreo.*

Fyre spoke into the silence. "You'll have to get married, you know."

The girl spun to face him. "What did you say, scale-face?"

He laughed. "Married. You. Or at least choose a mate to have children with. The strongest noble claims are the descendants of females."

"I think I have other problems at the moment, thanks. Talk to me in ten years." His irritating expression was filled with the knowledge that he was right and that he'd scored a point. She turned to the dresser with a growl of irritation and yanked on the bottom drawer with more force than was strictly necessary.

Her hand slipped and she landed on her rear end when it failed to budge. Her companion snorted once but wisely, didn't comment. She scooted to it and tried again, but it refused to move and when she released a trickle of magic, she sensed the ward protecting it. With her finger, she drew the rune that appeared in her mind on the surface of the drawer. The deactivation of the protective spell tasted like pineapple but triggered none of her other senses. *That's...weird.*

Cali pulled it open and found a variety of blades. The longest was a dagger that reached from the tip of her pinky to her elbow, the shortest barely as long as her hand. Each was held in a sheath marked with the house emblem, and the same image was etched into the weapons' metal and present on several of the hilts. The knives gleamed in the light, and the edges looked untouched by time or use. "Jenkins, what are these?"

"Ornamental arms, Matriarch Caliste, but no less deadly for it. Gatherings of the Nine permit only small blades, aside from the most formal occasions that allow swords. These, too, have been in the family for generations."

She replaced them in their container and slid it closed before she queried with her magic for the correct way to reactivate their protection and drew the appropriate rune.

Again, she tasted pineapple. With a groan, she pushed herself to her feet and crossed to the apothecary cabinet. Spreading her arms wide, she intoned, "Reveal your secrets," and pulled open the one on the lower right.

It took half an hour to examine them all, working her way from the outside in. The expected ornamental jewelry rested in some and papers that were too complex for a quick read in others. Empty vials, full vials without markings, stationery—the cabinet was a treasure trove of randomness.

But the two boxes she found made the whole exploration worthwhile. Each was subdivided into smaller compartments, and in each of those was a number of charms.

"Yes," she crowed as she retrieved one with the same symbol as the shield pendant that had been consumed. After a moment's thought, she collected two of those and one of each of the others for Emalia to examine. "Finally. Something immediately useful."

A noise far below sounded like a knock and Jenkins announced, "There is a messenger at the door from House Jehenel."

She frowned. "How do we feel about them?"

"House Leblanc has never been at odds with House Jehenel, but neither have they been counted among our allies." His use of the possessive brought a smile.

"All right, then. Let's see what he wants."

When she reached the bottom of the ladder, she used the same magic she'd employed earlier to raise it to its secure and closed position. She raced Fyre down the stairs and gained a head start before he knew they were competing. His wings gave him the necessary advantage, though, and he was seated at the front entrance when she arrived. She scowled. "I could have beat you with my magic."

He shook his head and his tongue lolled. "Hardly. I barely flapped."

"We'll have this out one day, short and snarly."

"Bring it."

Cali grinned and opened the door. On the porch stood a woman who seemed to be her own age, but that was all they had in common. She could have been a model with her tall, elegant looks and perfectly dressed hair that fell in soft brown waves to her shoulders. Her skin would have looked right on a beach at the end of summer, although her face was slightly more ordinary. The tight dress she wore—a dark purple sheath with pale yellow accents at the neck, cuffs, and down the sleeves—made Cali feel inappropriately informal.

Pushing down her immediate annoyance, she asked, "Yes?"

The visitor studied her with a haughty smile. "You're the matriarch of House Leblanc?" The way she emphasized the first word confirmed that this wouldn't be a pleasant interaction.

"Yeah. And you're a lackey, which on the whole is far less impressive, don't you think? Deliver your message, messenger."

Fyre sent amusement and she smothered a smile. The woman frowned and her voice lost any hint of warmth. "The patriarch of House Jehenel requests the pleasure of your company for an afternoon stroll at three o'clock."

She shrugged. "Sure. Tell him to come pick me up."

With a swing of her foot, she closed the door in the woman's face.

"Petty," the Draksa commented around a grin.

"Yeah, whatever. Now, I guess I need afternoon-stroll wear. Jenkins…"

Given that he was coming to her, it seemed only fair that she wait outside to greet him. She had found a decent pair of black pants among her mother's things and a long tunic, almost a dress, in turquoise with red accents. Elisinia's boots, which she kept in New Atlantis as a treat for when she visited, completed the outfit.

The man who walked down the sidewalk was even more handsome than the woman had been beautiful. While she'd dressed, Jenkins had given her details about him. The disembodied butler had been ready to provide a full history, but she'd told him to limit it to the recent past. Wymarc had been named patriarch a few years before and she'd now replaced him as the youngest head of a noble house. He had no particular focus but spent his time living well on the proceeds of his family's existing streams of income.

His walk was direct and confident, and he crossed the space to where she leaned against the doorjamb in short order. He smiled, showing flawless teeth. "Caliste, I presume?"

She nodded. "You presume correctly. And you're Wymarc."

"Indeed. Shall we?" He gestured toward the ring street

beyond the front fence of her property, and as she started in that direction, her escort fell into step beside her. It felt easy and natural, which made her immediately suspicious.

"So, you woke up this morning and said, 'Self, I think we need to meet the new girl on the block today. An afternoon walkabout is just the thing.' Is that it?"

He laughed and it was a decidedly attractive sound. "More or less. Have you listened to my internal voice somehow?"

A smile came unbidden to her lips. "Yes, that, definitely."

"Well, I guess you know all my secrets, then. You owe me some of your own in exchange. It's only fair."

Cali shook her head. "I may be dumb but I'm not that dumb."

They took the turn that would lead them toward the less affluent parts of town. He pointed at the mansion across the street from her own. "House Devaux. They are tricky buggers and not to be trusted."

She made a mental note to ask Jenkins whether that was accurate or not. With a nod, she replied, "And I suppose you are not tricky and are to be trusted?"

He shrugged. "You wouldn't be matriarch if you weren't able to make that decision for yourself. I'm simply here to give you the opportunity to know me better so you don't have to rely on rumors."

"And what kind of rumors might those be, Wymarc?"

He raised a finger. "First, that I am a cad and a womanizer. Second, that I am a dilettante who accomplishes what is somewhere in the middle of little and nothing. Finally, that I am exclusively concerned with my own comfortable existence and my family's interests."

As they walked, she had focused her gaze more or less ahead but now, she twisted her head to regard him curiously. "Are those rumors true?"

"Like most rumors, they probably contain a trace of truth. I do enjoy the company of women and there are a number who have enjoyed mine as well. I'm not a cad, though. I am fond of my lifestyle, although I also have things to focus on. I merely don't choose to be public about them all. And I am indeed concerned with comfort and the future of my family but not only that." He smiled. "And you? What rumors might I hear about you?"

Cali laughed. "Other than those that inspired you to walk with me, you mean?" He nodded. "I'm from New Orleans. There's a group there causing trouble for me, and the Malniets are my challenge here. My parents died before their time, like yours. There's not much else to tell."

He kept any derision out of his voice as he asked, "Is it true that you work at a restaurant?"

"It is, although tavern is a better word—heavy on the drink, light on the food."

"Well, this would be the perfect place for us to take a break, then." He gestured at a building on the opposite side of the ring street they'd reached. It had an image of an octopus holding several mugs of beer, and the picture was perfectly hilarious.

"Eight-fisted, huh? It's a clever name."

"We call it the eight because—you know, the Nine."

She rolled her eyes. "Yeah, I get it. Lead on." She followed him through the door and into the bar.

CHAPTER TWENTY-ONE

The interior was dark and a haze of smoke that wasn't identifiable as any kind of tobacco she'd been around hung in the air. It was filled with roughly an equal number of men and women, and those with pipes all seemed to be gathered at the rectangular bar. Two bartenders worked rapidly to pull drafts and pour wine. No mixed drinks were visible at all.

Booths were positioned on the outside walls with a walkway between them and the stools at the bar. Wymarc led her down the right-hand side to an empty booth and slid in. Cali peered carefully around the large room, looking for trouble under the guise of curiosity, but found none. She sat across from him.

Almost immediately, a server bustled up. He looked harried and annoyed but not at them in particular. If asked to guess, she would have put his age at a well-preserved fifty. His hair was going gray and it was cut short in a no-nonsense flattop. A raspy voice emerged from his round face. "What'll ya have?"

"Porter," Wymarc answered, and the older man nodded and turned to her.

"Uh, cider." He strode off without a reply. She didn't know what fruit or level of alcohol she'd be given, but it wasn't a cause for concern. Her plans didn't involve anything more than polite sips for flavor. While it might seem like a social occasion, she was as much at work as the server was.

"It was a good choice. They make great ones here." She attributed his faint smugness to putting her in a situation to choose a drink without knowing the territory. *Ah, so the competitiveness sneaks out. Excellent.*

She gave him an unassuming smile. "Wonderful. I can take any secrets home to my boss."

His lips turned down in a slight frown at the mention of her job. *Point for me. Your mask is slipping, friend.* Still, he'd done nothing to suggest his intentions were bad, only that he wasn't as pristine as he might have wanted to appear. She'd dealt with worse—Janice came to mind—but the thought vanished when he changed the subject abruptly.

"So, what can I tell you about your new home?" He raised his hands to indicate the surrounding area.

Cali chuckled. "New Atlantis isn't my home. Not yet, anyway. I've spent most of my formative years in New Orleans, and it's the kind of place that works its way into you. Have you traveled outside the dome much?"

He shrugged. "I've seen all that New Atlantis has to offer from the bright locations to the dark ones. Perhaps I should take a trip to the surface, though, one of these days.

Maybe you could show me around your town sometime."
He gave her a flirty grin.

"Sure. I'd be happy to. So what can you tell me about
this place that I don't know?"

The server deposited their drinks and left. She took a
sip and discovered that it was a highly potent apple-cherry
blend.

"Doubtless you already have information on the city as
a whole and on House Leblanc," Wymarc replied, "but
maybe not as much about the Nine. Most of them are okay,
but you have to watch Cormier and Surette." She was
surprised he hadn't added the Malniets to the list, if only
for the sake of credibility.

"Why is that?"

He scowled and sipped his beer. "Because they have a
long history of making alliances, only to break them in
moments of crisis. Say what you will about the other
houses, they at least tend to be consistent. If they dislike
you, they're clear about it and don't change that opinion
without generations of effort." He shook his head. "My
family has engaged with them both at times, and we'll never
make that particular mistake again. I'm sure they'll reach
out to you too in an attempt to influence your decisions."

She raised an eyebrow. "You mean like you're doing
today."

Her companion shrugged. "That's a possibility for
down the road. I'm not one to rush into things, so I'd call
this more an introduction than a solicitation."

Cali laughed. "I'm not sure I like the implication."

"No offense intended." He grinned. "It was a poor word

choice. My apologies." She nodded acceptance. "So, anyway, there are several ways to group the Nine, but the one I think is most accurate is pro-Shenni, neutral, and anti-Shenni."

"The Empress, you mean?"

"Exactly. Although the structure works no matter who holds the throne. The players merely move from cluster to cluster. She was a member of House Rivette before her ascension so obviously, they are in support. Oubre and Cormier as well. Against her—or maybe more accurately, for themselves above all—are Surette, Devaux, and your friends the Malniets. So, you see, your family and mine are likely to find ourselves working together to balance the other factions, along with House Terriau."

"Doesn't being neutral actually mean you support the monarch?"

He nodded. "To some degree. But there's support and there's *support*. The true loyalists would ignore an opportunity to remove her and of course, the anti-faction would embrace it. Those in the middle would judge each such situation individually. You might say, then, that we have the most power."

She smiled thinly, "And we will be the targets of the others every time they wish to swing our disposition one way or the other."

"Now you're getting it."

"So, if you had to guess what will happen in the short-term, what would it be?"

Wymarc laughed. "After meeting you today, I would imagine the next upheaval New Atlantis will face is the elimination of House Malniet."

They'd passed another pleasant hour together before Cali had said goodbye at his doorstep, which seemed only fair since she'd made him come to her house earlier. As she walked through the growing darkness, the details he'd given her settled into their proper places in her mind.

Allies, enemies, neutral. Pro-Shenni, anti-Shenni. Those looking to rise, those likely to fall. It was a jumble of concepts she'd never really considered in any other part of her life, and they all felt foreign. Even allies wasn't a comfortable term as she'd always used friend instead.

She entered the kitchen in search of the coffee that filled the air with its bitter aroma. Fyre headed for what had become his favorite corner, farthest from where her attempts at cooking took place. She poured herself a mug and sat at the table with Zeb and Emalia, who both looked smug. Cali glanced from one to the other and asked, "What?"

Her great aunt said, "Zeb improved all the wards. This place is as secure as can be."

"And Emalia gave all the outbuildings a quick search," her boss added. "There's nothing there that requires your immediate attention. I'll wander over and improve their protections before we leave."

There was something more in their attitudes, though. Each of them had played jokes on her enough that she knew the signs. She put her hands on her hips with a frown. "Okay, what aren't you telling me?"

Zeb broke into a grin and gestured at Emalia. "I've decoded part of the book your parents left you. We know where one of the sword shards is."

Stunned, she sat in silence for a few moments, then uttered a loud whoop. "Awesome! Where is it?"

"It's hidden on Oriceran."

"Did they say why?"

"Not yet. I started at the drawing of the sword you marked and worked in both directions from there. I'd only translated a couple of pages before I found the reference but I'll keep working on it."

Cali nodded. "And the other charms?" A new shield pendant hung from her neck but she didn't know how to activate the others yet.

Her great aunt laughed. "Yes, and that too. You're quite the taskmaster."

She rose with a grin. "You gotta earn your keep somehow, lady."

The dwarf's gaze followed her. "And so do you. We need to get back, don't you think?"

"Yep. I have one thing left to take care of and we'll be good to go."

She refilled her coffee and hurried to the first-floor den, which had been her parents' office as far as she could tell. Once seated behind the desk that contained the stationery and the wax, she retrieved some of each. The center drawer produced a pen, and she thought about how to properly phrase the invitation she was about to draft.

A frown of concentration appeared as she focused on making the handwriting legible.

To: Patriarch Styrris, House Malniet.

In keeping with the rituals of New Atlantis, I summon two champions to face the same from House Leblanc, four days hence at eight in the evening at the same location as before. Of course, if you wish to acknowledge your ultimate defeat and offer me the boon I seek, that would certainly be an acceptable outcome as well.

Signed,

Caliste, Matriarch of House Leblanc.

She looked at Fyre. "Would it be wrong to add a post-script? Something like 'Oh, and by the way, you and your family are all jerks who deserve to live neck-deep in an anthill forever?'"

He snorted. "That would perhaps be a little too on the nose, all things considered."

"Yeah, I guess so." She nodded reluctantly. "Hey, Jenkins?"

The spirit replied from the corner of the room. "Yes, Matriarch Caliste?"

"Can you and Emalia arrange for this to be delivered before the end of the day?"

"Indeed so."

"Thanks." She rose and stretched. "Okay, buddy, I think it's time we headed to New Orleans. We can make sure Janice hasn't burned the tavern down in our absence, get our things together to search for a sword, and check on Dasante and Tanyith." He trotted at her side as she returned to the kitchen.

Zeb stood when she arrived, clearly ready to go. She nudged the Draksa with her leg. "See? He's worried about her burning it down, too."

He growled in annoyance. "I am not. Don't pick on Janice. It's unseemly, Matriarch."

Cali laughed. "Oh, heaven forbid I do something

unseemly." She gestured with her arms to create a portal with the basement of the Drunken Dragons on the opposite side. "Emalia, is everything good with you? I should be back Monday."

Her great aunt nodded. "If any problems arise, I'll lock myself in and wait. But I'm sure it'll be fine."

"Trust no one. Especially Wymarc Jehenel."

"Oh? You two aren't engaged yet?"

She rolled her eyes. "Yep, time to go. The people here are simply annoying." With a smile, she stepped through.

CHAPTER TWENTY-TWO

As he strode across the threshold into his tavern, Zeb heaved a happy sigh. More than his actual house, this place felt like home to him. He'd been glib about Janice but in truth, he hadn't liked leaving someone other than him in charge, even for only the couple days they'd been gone. He couldn't imagine anyone else—other than maybe his brother on Oriceran—who would have been able to convince him to do so.

But Cali held a special place in his heart and he would do almost anything for her.

Except the thing you're best at, his inner voice countered. The dwarf shook his head and climbed the stairs at Cali's heels. The Thursday night crowd was smaller than usual, but that wasn't a shock since Janice was running the tavern alone. A cheer went up at his arrival, and his temporary replacement grinned as she ducked out from behind the bar to give him a hug. "We survived, but things are always better when the boss is here."

Cali sounded like she made an effort to be pleasant

when she said, "Thank you, Janice. It was really nice of you to take over to free him up."

The other woman nodded. "Do you two have it from here?"

Zeb turned to confirm it with the snarky redhead, but she had already strode into the crowd. He laughed. "Yep, it's all good. Thanks again."

Janice grinned and headed toward the exit, saying farewells to the folks at the bar. He took his place and lost himself in work for a while, the familiar rhythms soothing. Before he realized how much time had passed, the moment had arrived to start pushing the patrons out the door.

Once they were all gone and the entrance was locked against new customers, Cali climbed onto a stool and put her head on the surface of the bar. "Damn, I'm tired."

He slid a soft cider beside her hand and it took her almost a full minute to look up again. When she did, the strain was visible on her features, especially around her eyes.

"You have every right to be," he said softly. "Things have changed dramatically for you in the last few months."

Her fingers trembled as she reached for the glass, but she managed to down half the drink without spilling it. She was a little more herself when she finished and summoned a wry grin. "Yeah. Who would have thought I'd have a legacy to live up to?"

He chuckled. "You've already done that. I have zero doubt you're every inch the person your parents hoped you would be and more. Now, it's all gravy, adding your volume to the story of the Noble House of Leblanc."

She snorted. "Hah. Noble. I think I like being known as your server more than by such a lofty title."

"You're both. That's what makes you special. It's what will enable you to beat any of those luxury-raised morons who try to attack you."

"I'm not quite as confident about that as you are."

"You should be. I'm very knowledgeable about such things."

Cali laughed. "I'm sure Valerie was the brains of the operation."

He looked over his shoulder at the battle-ax. "We were more like partners, actually."

"Are you saying that Valerie is an artifact?" She raised an eyebrow.

Zeb shook his head. "You can go now. It's time to close."

"You're deflecting."

"I'll see you tomorrow for work. Shoo."

She drained her glass and pointed a finger at him. "This conversation isn't over."

He waved and she departed. The fact that he'd put a smile on her face counted, though, and he gave himself a mental pat on the back for his cleverness.

It's time to get out of here and hit the rack. Tomorrow will come early.

Zeb stood outside the front door and sketched a symbol in the air to set the physical locks and activate the magical wards on the building before he stuck his pipe between his lips. He cupped his hand over the bowl and sparked it with a match, then drew deep and expelled the smoke through his nose.

His pipe leaf was another constant reminder of Oriceran, a touchstone that kept his past and present connected to each other. His life had changed since he'd come to Earth, but he hadn't, not really.

Oh sure, his inner voice commented. *Go ahead and lie to yourself.*

"Shut it." He growled under his breath and set off for home. His house was only a few blocks away, too close for portaling to be worth the effort. Besides, the walks were another ritual that calmed him and helped him to keep his mind in the right place—one other than the violence that had captured so many of his early days. Back then, he'd felt like it would overcome him. Now, however, he thought he would probably have learned to adapt. Either way, he liked his life as it was, and as long as Cali was around, he saw no reason for change. If she decided to make New Atlantis her permanent home, he might consider joining her for a while, simply for the new experiences.

His internal musing occupied him enough that when two tall Atlanteans in hoodies and jeans stepped from the corner into his path, it came as a surprise. It took only a moment for his senses to kick into gear and identify the sounds of several more trailing him, and the tactical voice in his mind anticipated the presence of at least one more in reserve ahead. Zeb removed his pipe and pointed it calmly at the duo in front of him. "You're not really this stupid, are you?"

They laughed, and the sound was echoed from behind him. The one on the right replied. "We're not the ones walking alone at night. Maybe you should have thought your decision to support the girl through a little more. Choices like that have ramifications." He said the final word like he was proud to know it and possibly understood what it meant.

The dwarf sighed. "Okay, you've delivered your threat. I am duly cowed. If you're smart, you'll shove off now."

The one on the left shook his head. "Do you think we're scared of your friend? Even if we were, she's not here right now."

He shrugged. "This is your last chance. You should consider the ramifications of your next move carefully."

The two in front didn't react, but the scuff of a shoe behind him telegraphed the incoming attack. Zeb darted to his left, dropped into a deep crouch, and spun to his right. The metal bar that had been swung at his head pounded into the concrete where he'd stood and drew a wince from the man who'd made the attempt to fell him. A second man and a woman now stalked toward him, the former holding a baseball bat and the latter an unexpectedly large blade. It took him a moment to place it.

Where the blazes did she find a bayonet?

He noted the positions of everyone around him casually, including the extra man in the front.

Six on one. At least they realized I wouldn't be a pushover.

He calculated that he had time to deal with the two from the rear before the others reached him. Swiftly, he moved to close the distance between them and circled to his right to put the woman in the way of the man with the bat. She swiped at him with the bayonet and he growled his disapproval.

"That's a stabbing weapon, fool," he told her and let the blade move past her centerline, then stepped in and raised his right hand to grasp her elbow. He punched up into the bottom of her bicep with his left hand to numb the arm, then drove the same fist into her ribs. They snapped and she clutched them as she fell.

The bat already swung viciously so he darted back to let it pass. He backpedaled to keep his enemies all on one side as the three from the front joined the attack. The man who'd spoken to him first glowered at him. "Screw it. We had planned to only give you a beating but now, you get the full treatment."

Zeb had slipped into what he thought of as his fighting mode. It had been years since he'd practiced with any serious intent since he'd taken the intentional decision to leave that way of life behind him. A conviction that his cause was right and just flowed through him to banish most thoughts other than those of victory. In the past, it had banished all thoughts, but he'd spent the time between then and now working to improve his mind and deepen his self-understanding. He was able to partition one small section to provide guidance to the rest, something important he'd previously lacked. It reminded him there was no need to kill in this situation, only to injure.

The feeling of his forearm cuffs flowing over his hands without conscious instruction was a shock of cold magic that made his skin crawl for a moment, but it passed quickly and the viscous liquid solidified into his magical weapons. They had been the inspiration for those he'd crafted for Cali, mostly as a way to pass the time after they'd met. He'd never imagined she'd actually need them.

His hatchets featured three impact surfaces. The head of the weapon had a curved blade on one side and a blunt knob on the other, and the base of the shaft had a flat-bottomed metal ball on it. They weren't weighted for throwing as such, but he'd had enough practice that he was more than proficient at it. They would return to him with a thought and a trickle of magic. More than that, though, the weapons were a conduit for his own magics, which operated practically without conscious direction when the combat axes were in his hands.

If only I had my armor.

You don't need it for this group, his inner voice almost crowed in reply. He echoed the statement out loud. "You're right, I don't need it for them."

The Atlanteans had taken a step back when the weapons appeared but seemed to have gathered their wits. He clapped the heads of the hatchets together and as the metal chimed, a wave of force flowed from them. The two who had been the first to speak managed to summon shields quickly enough to hold their ground, but the others were hurled from their feet.

"Well, all right then," he said and smiled. "Let's see what you have."

They attacked together, which demonstrated a measure of sense. The one on the left ejected a cone of flame at him, while the one on the right tried shadow bolts that streaked across the distance between them. He shuffled to the left to avoid the dark magic and raised his hatchet to intercept the fire. The head of the weapon glowed as his magic drew the flames in and the metal portion gleamed cherry-red. After several seconds, the man let the ineffective attack fall away. Zeb smiled and charged.

Most people assumed that because dwarves lacked height, they were also slow. The assumption was, of course, incorrect but had proved useful as an element of surprise. As he'd once told Cali, he was a sprinter, not a marathoner and over short distances, he was wickedly fast. He was beside the two men before they realized it and spun his hatchets so the blunt part of the head faced them. As he raced between them, he channeled his momentum and his strength into the weapons held at arm's length and drove the metal knobs into their stomachs.

Both collapsed without a sound other than sharp exhalations of breath. He had a moment to hope he'd pulled the blow enough to not permanently injure them before the remaining three made their attempt.

The bat-wielder came in first, and it was a simple matter to block his downward strike with one hatchet. Zeb pointed his weapon at the other man, and a snapping sound accompanied the sizzle of lightning that erupted from the head to wreath the man in electricity. He danced involuntarily for a moment before he fell.

While the dwarf had been occupied with the others, the one with the metal bar had closed enough to whip it at his stomach. Zeb jumped back and took the strike, which was now weakened by the distance, then slammed both his hatchets down to knock the weapon out of his foe's hands.

The man looked at him, wide-eyed, and he resisted the urge to hurl a blade at his face. He shook his head. "Get along now. Go." He pointed his left-hand weapon at the last man, who'd attempted to sneak around him. "Uh-uh.

You go too—right this second or you'll both go down permanently. And tell your masters that if they come after me or any of Cali's friends again, they're asking for way more trouble than they know how to handle."

The sneaky one raised his palms and backpedaled before the duo turned and ran. Zeb shook his head at the idiots. He envisioned the throws that would put his blades in their backs, but the controlled portion of his mind prevented the weapons from leaving his hands. Turning to check on the others, he found them damaged but alive. He retrieved the phone he denied having from the secret pocket in his trousers and dialed the police tip line with the location.

That done, the dwarf let his hatchets flow into their hidden state and walked home, whistling in the dark.

CHAPTER TWENTY-THREE

Cali sealed her uniform, then slotted her potions into place in her thigh pouches. After she'd seen the leather sheaths her mother had packed away, the idea of something similar for the metal vials that contained her healing and energy brews had occurred to her, but there hadn't yet been time to make it happen.

The smarter move would have been to wait a few days before she began the search for the sword piece Emalia had found, but she wasn't able to cope with any further delay. With each day that passed, her need to bring the mysteries surrounding her parents and their deaths to a resolution grew exponentially. At times, it was almost suffocating and the only way to deal with it was to keep moving forward.

Like a shark. Swim or die.

Which was why she, Tanyith, and Fyre were in the bunker early on a Saturday morning, gearing up for a treasure hunt. At least that's what he had called it, and she couldn't argue the point. The Draksa paced, more agitated than she'd seen him in the recent past.

"What's the deal, buddy? Are you okay?"

He growled. "Still mad about the attack."

She nodded. Zeb had called from the tavern early that morning to let her know that the Atlanteans had attacked him the night before. He sounded none the worse for wear and in fact, he'd seemed almost happy about it. The idea that her friends remained in danger apparently offended Fyre almost as much as it did her, however. "I hear you, but one problem at a time. They'll get theirs."

He muttered something she wasn't able to hear and continued to pace. Tanyith distracted her from that worry by introducing another. "I realized the last time I was in here that there aren't any weapons around. It seems weird that your parents wouldn't have had them, don't you think? We only know about the one sword, but there has to be other stuff."

Cali paused while lacing her boots to consider the statement. It did make sense that they'd have others, but she hadn't seen any sign of them anywhere aside from the ornamental ones at the Leblanc estate. "That's a good point but I have no idea where to start looking. Maybe Emalia will discover something in the coded book." She tied the final lace. "Anyway, it's a problem for another day. Let's put our game faces on and find some treasure."

They met Invel in the main room of the Drunken Dragons at ten am, as arranged. When they climbed the stairs from the basement, he was drinking a soft cider at the bar and gossiping with Zeb, who looked inordinately pleased with himself.

He's probably telling the story of the attack. Drama queen. "All right, you two, let's get a move on," she called, and the Drow laughed as he stood and limped toward her.

Her boss tilted his chin in her direction. "Back to the basement. I've given him access."

They walked down together, chatting about unimportant things. At the bottom, Invel asked, "So, how is Emalia faring?"

Cali suppressed her grin. "She's doing quite well and New Atlantis seems to suit her. I'll return there on Monday. If you'd like to come for a visit, you're certainly welcome to join me."

He gave her a small smile. "I'd enjoy that very much."

"Done deal. You know, assuming I make it from Oriceran alive."

Immediately, his expression turned serious. "The area where you're going has a history filled with tales of danger and death."

"You take us to the best places, Cali," Tanyith quipped. "You're a really great friend to have."

She tried and failed to glare at him and contented herself with her old standby. "Shut it." To Invel, she said, "I appreciate the warning, but I have to go where the path leads. I owe it to my parents and to my house, but mostly to myself. I have to know."

He nodded. "I understand. So, due east from where you step through." He'd provided her with a compass that worked on the other planet to help her find her way and had shown her a map of the area. It was direct enough, merely a couple of miles of uneven but unobstructed terrain between the place he knew and where the entrance to the cave should be.

It'll be simple. Easy. We've got this. "Thanks for everything."

He nodded and summoned the portal. She jumped through before she could reconsider whether it was a good idea or not.

Sunlight baked onto her from the moment she emerged and made her eyes water. The surrounding area was grassland, with trees on the horizon in three directions and a mountain directly ahead of them. She raised a hand to her forehead to shade her vision and checked the compass strapped to her forearm. "This way." Without hesitation, she strode forward and her companions followed.

"So, did Emalia find out anything about how the shard got here?" Tanyith asked.

She nodded. "One of the other houses, apparently being clever, but she didn't know which. It seems they really like playing games against each other. Everything's a challenge or a competition. So essentially, this wasn't technically 'stealing' or 'trying to kill us,' but only a little adventure to see if they're better at the game than we are."

"That's idiotic."

Cali laughed. "Yeah, that's one way to look at it. I suppose it makes sense if you were raised into it. Or something." She shook her head. "Okay, I have no idea how this might make sense. The noble houses are freakin' weird."

Fyre snorted. "Yours is no exception."

"Quiet you." They plodded along in silence for a half-hour, except to point out potentially dangerous places where the ground looked uncertain. Finally, they arrived at the location Invel had instructed them to find, a thin crack that marked the entrance of a cave.

Tanyith shook his head. "That looks like a trap if ever I saw one. How did Emalia find this place again?"

"Oh, the other house told my parents where it was. It's part of the challenge."

"So yes, trap," Fyre replied.

"Almost certainly." She nodded. "But I bet we're better than they are."

Cali held her breath as she slipped through the crevice and her skin crawled as magic washed over her. A moment later, she pushed through into a small chamber. She summoned a ball of fire and tossed it up to hover far enough away from the walls and ceiling that she wouldn't accidentally set anything alight.

I definitely need to work on my lightning magic. "It's safe. Come on through." Fyre was next and stood on his hind legs to fit, but his expected entrance didn't materialize.

He snarled in frustration. "I'm blocked. Magic. Can't get in."

She frowned. "Maybe it's a barrier to Draksa? Or creatures who are fundamentally magical?"

"Probably not," Tanyith replied. "I can't get in either."

"It has to be tied somehow to House Leblanc, then." She sighed. "Those bastards. It makes sense, though, for the purposes of the game." She muttered a curse or two and looked at the exit. "I can't leave now. I'm too close. You two try to find another way in and I'll push on." They hadn't brought the comms as they assumed they'd be together and were doubtful that the devices would work on Oriceran in any case. "Fyre can keep us connected. Be careful."

The Draksa rumbled, obviously disapproving of the situation. "You be careful. There's no telling what these scumbags left behind for you."

"Yeah. Will do." She turned to face the other exit from the room, a small hole on the far side she'd have to crawl through. "Okay. Here we go." She sent the fireball into the gap, now willing to set anything that annoyed her alight. It revealed a tunnel that extended farther than she could see. With a sigh, she lowered herself to her hands and knees and ducked through the opening.

Once I find out which house did this, I'll make a special point of kicking the asses of the entire family line.

CHAPTER TWENTY-FOUR

After several minutes of crawling and cursing, Cali emerged in a large chamber. Nothing thus far had seemed crafted and it appeared that whoever had set the game up had simply used the natural cave features to their advantage. Even though she hadn't sensed a descent, this room felt like it was underground, with stalactites above and a thin line of water that meandered along a shallow channel from one wall to the other.

On the opposite side was another crack that looked similar to the one she'd entered the mountain through, but this one was thankfully a little wider. She took a step toward it but stopped cold.

Wait, it's too easy. Get your head on straight, Cali.

She swept her gaze systematically across the chamber in search of obvious traps but found none. With a deep breath, she let her magic trickle forth. Often, of late, she didn't know quite what she was doing and simply allowed it to flow with the intention of discovery behind it. When it reached the water, anise exploded on her tongue and she gagged from the intensity. The liquid glowed, both in the channel and where the surrounding stone was damp.

"Okay, that can't be good." She used her force magic to coat the floor of the cavern and trap the dangerous water beneath it. Once she'd locked that into place in a corner of her mind, she sent her power questing again. It found nothing else, so she crossed the space carefully and squeezed into the crack. Only when she was safely though did she release the former spell before she crouched to examine the next area.

Where the last area had been wide, this one was narrow and long, with two obvious exits on the far side. Two statues that looked uncomfortably like Atlantean enforcers separated the chamber into thirds, which left very little room to move past them on either side. The ceiling was high but stalactites stabbed down at random intervals to make flight a dicey proposition, especially given her general lack of finesse.

Decisions, decisions. What would I do if I was a jerkwad noble trying to kill an intruder?

The answer was uncomfortably simple—both routes were probably trapped. She trickled a thread of magic to search above and it returned a faint taste of anise. When she did the same with the statues, though, she received a much more prominent warning. The one closest to her lurched into motion, its stone suddenly as supple as flesh, and hurled a net at her.

Cali screamed in alarm and flung herself forward to pass under the net. The good news was that the statue blocked the other one from engaging her. The bad news was that it had drawn a large, two-handed sword and now strode toward her, its blank and lifeless eyes somehow menacing. She summoned her sticks and raised them in time to manage an X-block against a diagonal sword cut but had nowhere to go to avoid the front kick that followed. The reinforced jacket helped to dull the blow to her stomach but it still hurled her back several feet.

As soon as her boots touched the stony surface, she immediately ran forward and slid under another diagonal slash, then slammed her sticks into her attacker's knees. Her hands ached from the impact, which seemed to accomplish nothing. She considered sneaking past, but the trident that stabbed at her between the first statue's legs quickly disabused her of that notion. As she scrambled away, she let her right-hand stick transform into a bracelet again.

She glanced at the ceiling in preparation to launch herself to the far end regardless of the danger when she saw an opportunity. Raising her fist, she discharged a force blast and cracked a stalactite. It fell, impaled the statue beneath it, and shattered it into rocks. She did the same with those closest to the second one and grinned in satisfaction as it succumbed to the sharp missiles.

Her smile was banished by a cracking sound from above. Cali sprinted to the opposite side, chose the left opening at random, and dove through it a second before the ceiling caved in behind her. She sat and panted for several moments, then realized she received waves of worry from Fyre over their mental connection.

"I'm safe, no worries," she said. "Relax, buddy." The intensity diminished a little. "Have you found a way in?"

She could almost hear the growl in the surge of

emotion that followed and she chuckled darkly. "Okay, keep trying and be alert. Their traps are magical and overlapping so far." He didn't send a specific reply, only a continued thread of concern.

Yeah. I'm a little worried too, to be honest. She summoned a small sphere of fire and rolled it along the ground down the passage. It illuminated a tunnel tall enough to walk in but too narrow for her to extend her arms at all. For better or worse, it sloped downward. Her instincts warned her that more dangerous obstacles likely lay below, and she assumed that probably meant the treasure did too.

Cali pushed herself up with a sigh and summoned her second stick again. She'd need every advantage possible if trouble manifested in the claustrophobic corridor. Her senses screamed caution as she crept ahead one step at a time and made sure to keep her weight on her back leg in case the ground below should prove uncertain. The tunnel ended in a room that had clearly not been created by nature. It was both long and wide, with pillars down the left and right sides to create an obvious walkway down the middle. Magical lanterns glowed, and she banished her unnecessary flame. Heavy stone blocks the color of sand formed the walls, engraved with symbols, runes, and designs she couldn't identify.

At the end of the central path was what appeared to be an altar, and on it was a shining silver object, aglow in the crossbeams from three lanterns. Even from this distance, the runes were visible. The floor was made up of smaller blocks that resembled those in the walls with a different symbol etched into each.

When she looked up, the ceiling wasn't as high as she

assumed it would be. There was no doubt in her mind that a plethora of tricks, traps, and magical defenses stood between her and the shard.

"I'm in some kind of fancy room," she sent to Fyre. "The sword piece is on the other side." He returned caution to her, and she nodded. "Yeah, I know. I don't trust anything in here."

Her magic sensed danger all around, filled her mouth with the taste of black licorice, and gave her nothing specific enough to be useful. She remained where she'd stopped on entry, which was a single large block bordered by the smaller ones that stretched through the room. It was too far to launch herself, given the height of the ceiling. She'd need more of an arc than the available space would permit.

After a few moments of focused thought, she transformed her sticks into a jo staff and stabbed it at the blocks in front of her. One after the next, they crumbled until she found one that didn't. She extended it to the next row and did the same thing. The discovery that the same symbol acted differently frustrated her, but she gritted her teeth and continued to test each one. Before long, she'd worked those ahead of her as far as three rows deep, but her staff wouldn't reach any further.

Okay, it's time to give this a try. She stepped onto the first and it wobbled beneath her but held. She stopped to catch her breath.

I should throw a force barrier over the whole thing and walk on that. As soon as it crossed her mind, she discarded the idea. While that might have worked on the initial trap, which likely relied on secrecy, they'd surely have considered that solution in the construction of this challenge. She could picture the ceiling falling or something equally catastrophic in response. A quick involuntary look upward confirmed that it was still stable, and she stepped onto the next block. She continued to test and step until she reached a set of tiles with a golden border on the near side.

Every game has clues, and this has to be one. Something probably changes after this.

Cali poked at the blocks ahead with the staff, but they didn't seem to react in the least. With a frown, she commanded the sticks to return to bracelet form and summoned a force shield sufficient to cover her from head to toe in each hand. She'd seen enough movies to know the risks that came with tomb raiding, and while this might not be a tomb, it definitely possessed a funereal feel. She crept forward slowly, keeping her weight balanced, but nothing happened to alarm her. Cautiously, she stepped across a few more blocks, holding the shields to either side so she was almost cocooned.

With a creak and a crash, the surface behind her fell away. She didn't wait to see where it had gone and simply sprinted ahead. Arrows fired from the walls on both sides, but her shields protected her from the impacts. Her attention faltered for a moment, but she shored it up, then shrieked when a giant ax swung at her from above. She did the only thing possible to avoid having her skull split in half and slid under it but the back of her head rapped on the stone as she landed.

Had she not been dazed, there might have been time to react to the part of the floor that suddenly tipped as she landed. As it was, all she could do was add another yelp when she plunged into the darkness and shouted, "*Aspida*," to activate her shield necklace.

She pulled the shields in her hands inward until they touched, willed them to join together, and hoped for the best as she fell.

CHAPTER TWENTY-FIVE

While it felt like an hour, it was probably only seconds before her descent was halted by the sound of shattering wood and grinding metal. She waited to see if anything else happened for at least another hour-seeming minute. When nothing manifested, she let the protective cocoon generated by her necklace dissipate. She settled a little lower and at an angle, but no further danger appeared.

The shield beneath her was attached to her left hand, so she curled into it, dispelled the right one, and summoned a tiny fireball in its place that she tossed into the air. It was light enough that it rose toward the ceiling. The flickering light revealed that she was in a wide pit lined with half-sized spears. Her shield had saved her from the points and her weight had broken their wooden supports. She shook her head.

"That could have been bad." She didn't sense anything from Fyre but sent him a message that she was okay.

Sometimes, when she got worked up, the connection between them was drowned out by her own concerns.

She stood and let her shield fall before she conjured a couple more fireballs and tossed them into the corners. The pit appeared to have no exits other than the top, which had closed after she'd plunged through it. "Clever bastards. I'll definitely find out who you are and introduce you to one of my favorite games. I call it 'run like hell or get your legs broken.'" She continued to babble to herself as she looked around for options.

The walls were block, similar to those above but smaller with lines of mortar between the courses. *That's a possibility.* She bent and retrieved one of the cracked spears that had a foot or so of wood left attached to the head. Her teeth gritted, she thrust it into the mortar at chest height, but all it did was chip the material slightly. With a growl of frustration, she drove it in again and again until it was stuck in place, then nodded.

Okay, at least I know it will work as a Plan B. She used force magic to snap off as many of the remaining spears as would comfortably fit in her belt but still allow her to move.

Cali checked to ensure her potions were where they were supposed to be because if she faltered, things would get ugly. She tried to think back to how she'd fallen but wasn't able to recall what had actually happened. If the opposite side of the cover had gone up, it meant a crossbar support in the middle of a tilting platform. On the other hand, it might have hinges at the far end. She was fifty-one percent sure it was the former, so she decided to go up on the side that would lift at the top if she was correct.

Her magic coalesced into a set of force stairs, which reminded her of one of her first clumsy attempts at the technique shortly before she'd met Fyre. So much had changed since those days, to be sure. She made it about halfway up before the next stair refused to form.

So, something is blocking magic, which I suppose is logical and even necessary from their perspective. Jerks. She turned and jammed the spears into the wall one after another, then climbed them to position higher ones. Finally, she reached the top and pushed on the lid. It shifted an inch but no more. With a growl of annoyance, she shoved harder and the spear beneath her feet wobbled alarmingly.

She paused to catch her balance, ready to jump into the open space below if there was no other option. Her support held, and she sent her thanks out to the universe.

"One more break. That's all I need." *The anti-magic spell or device or whatever it is might be set up to react to the presence of magic. If I'm lucky, that doesn't include magic that stays inside the body.*

Cali withdrew her energy potion slowly, drank it, and the power spread through her like a hot drink on a freezing day. She pushed it into her muscles and readied herself for her next attempt.

When she was ready, she kicked the wall to either side of the spear she stood on and most of the way up toward the lid to create holes for her feet that would be more stable than standing on one of the protrusions. She stabbed a spear near the top to use as a handhold, then climbed so her back was rounded against the barrier that separated her from the room upstairs.

With a shout, she lurched upward with all her might.

The lid lifted a foot, which gave her the space to jam a spear at an angle between it and the floor. She positioned several more and clambered through the opening she'd made, then rolled over to stare at the ceiling as she panted with exhaustion and relief.

Fyre's concern washed over her, and she returned giddy laughter. "It tried to kill me, buddy, but I'm okay. I don't suppose y'all are any closer to finding me, are you?" What he sent back didn't feel like a positive response. She shrugged. "It's fine. It seems as if it would be against the rules to not have a way out, so as long as I can steer clear of the traps, I should be able to get the shard and find a door or something."

She climbed slowly to her feet and the pain reminded her of the strain she'd put her body under. Before she continued, she retrieved a healing potion and drank a fourth of it to undo whatever damage had been inflicted.

"Okay. I'm halfway there." She was, however, now at the right distance to avoid the ground entirely and took almost a full minute to scan the ceiling to ensure there weren't any surprises waiting for her. Finally, she decided to hedge her bets, stated, "*Aspida*," and launched herself in an arc toward the table at the far end and the sword shard that lay upon it. Stalactites fell and bounced off her shield, and both fire and electrical attacks surged from the columns she passed, but the protective legacy her parents had left for her was adequate to defend against them all.

Cali landed on the raised platform that held the table and banished the shield. The opening scene from Raiders of the Lost Ark played in her mind, and she hoped to not find a gigantic boulder awaiting her. She wrapped her hands in force magic and grasped the blade. Nothing happened for the first moment, then a grinding sound issued from the wall in front of her. It lifted to reveal a passage. She shook her head. "Nope. No way. I've had enough."

She attempted to summon a portal and was half-shocked when the spell completed and the outside of the mountain was revealed. Before anything could go wrong, she ran through it and a surge of happiness from Fyre streamed across their connection.

It took them a dozen minutes to find each other and another ten to compare stories. When she'd regained enough energy for the spell, they returned to the basement of the Drunken Dragons. They climbed the stairs together, Cali barely able to put one foot in front of the other, and claimed seats at the bar. She looked at her watch and saw that she had exactly an hour before her shift started. With a sigh, she handed the blade to Zeb. "Put that somewhere and wake me in fifty-five minutes."

He shook his head. "You'll need to shower before you work, girl. You look like you've been swimming in a swamp."

"Fifty minutes, then," she mumbled, already on her way into unconsciousness.

CHAPTER TWENTY-SIX

After work the night before, Cali had returned to the bunker and stored the shard safely before she collapsed for twelve hours of blissful sleep. She'd bounced out of bed in the early afternoon filled with energy. Frye wasn't nearly as peppy and looked at her with one eye open while she raced around getting ready. Finally, when her hair was clean, conditioned, and properly wrangled and she was dressed in her favorite jean shorts and t-shirt, she poked him.

"Let's go, lazybones. We're taking a walk."

With a growl that changed pitch as he stretched, the Draksa jumped to the floor. A ripple formed around him as the illusion took hold and he became a Rottweiler to everyone but her. She opened the front door and he dashed through. The sun glowed fiercely beyond the confines of the building, and she squinted and slipped on a pair of gaudy white plastic sunglasses.

He looked over his shoulder and smirked. "I didn't know you were an Elton John impersonator."

"Shut it, you." She rolled her neck and stretched her arms over her head, then bent to touch the ground with her palms. "Okay, let's keep it under a brisk walk. I don't want to be all sweaty when we see Scoppic." It was a dozen blocks or so to the library, and she kept her gaze moving and her mind open in case a threat should appear unexpectedly. Fortunately, none did, and she was soon inside the air-conditioned splendor of one of her favorite places.

It was quiet and only a few students and about the same number of adults worked at tables, while a handful more made their way through the shelves of books. The visible staff was all human, and each gave her a smile as she passed through the huge, well-lit room. She had spent many hours there doing schoolwork or simply hiding out from the rest of the world before she discovered the full extent of her magical ability. In all that time, she'd never paid attention to the door she headed to now.

It lay at the back of the large first floor and claimed to be only for staff. She knew the proper words and magics to defeat the wards, however, and in moments, she entered the arcane library that existed beneath the public one. Three levels high, the expansive space was a cross between an elegant living room and a work of modern art with glass stairs, bookshelves on the walls reaching to the ceiling, and scattered desks, couches, chairs, and tables. It was one of the most beautiful places she'd ever seen and was also the frequent domain of the gnome, Scoppic, who was as pleasant and encouraging as the library was impressive.

She found him at his desk at the rear of the middle level, with a tower of books stacked on a side of the wooden surface. He broke into a grin at their appearance.

"Fyre, Caliste, welcome back!" Thus far, he'd given her no reason to believe that his enthusiastic goodwill was anything other than genuine.

Cali sat across from him, and the Draksa walked in a circle once beside the desk, then lay where the librarian could see him. On an earlier visit, Scoppic had been very excited to meet one of the creatures in the real world that he'd only read about previously, and Fyre had basked in his appreciation.

"You are such a glutton for attention," she sent and received mirth over their mental connection.

She looked at the gnome. "So, I had a few questions I wondered if you could help me with."

He nodded. "It's what I do, Matriarch." He laughed. "Such an exciting time for you, being named leader of your house!"

His sincerity was undeniable, and she had no wish to quash it. "Exciting is a good word for it." She chuckled. "Actually, that's part of the reason I'm here. I've discovered that a member of my line was once exposed to a certain poison. Because of the danger of it happening again, I'm looking for any records that might exist of magical poisons, especially those from Atlantis Old or New."

He tapped a finger against the desk and remained silent for half a minute, then brightened. "I don't have much on New Atlantean poison craft, but we do have a copy of the book that's considered to be the definitive work on potions, which also includes poisons." He gestured for her to rise and led her and the Draksa down a flight of stairs to the base of one of the bookshelves. He looked up, and she did the same. "Up there...the red spine. Do you see it?"

She did, but her telekinetic abilities were limited enough that she'd probably bring down the whole shelf if she tried to retrieve the tome in the usual manner. "Oh, I can see it but I can't reach it. I could send Fyre up, but his claws are fairly sharp."

A look of horror appeared on his face in the moment before he realized she was kidding, then vanished under a smile. "Very funny, Caliste. Very funny indeed." He raised a palm and the book slid out from the shelves and descended to hover above at chest height.

Quickly, she caught the oversized tome and hugged it to her chest. "Thank you, as always. I'll spend some time with this and see you if I have additional questions if that's all right."

"Of course. Please do." He moved away to do something else on the bottom level, and she climbed the stairs to a desk large enough to hold the book. She set it down softly to avoid making noise and bothering the other patrons who circulated quietly throughout the magical library before she glanced at Fyre. "If I'd known this place existed a year ago, I would have spent all my time here."

He smiled but chose not to respond and instead, curled under the desk. She hadn't had an opportunity to research it but had warmed to the belief that most Draksa wouldn't or couldn't talk. Nylotte had said that Fyre was different and perhaps that was why. In any case, it didn't matter as long as her partner remained happy and safe.

Cali turned her attention to the book. It was written longhand in a sweeping and beautiful style. A vague hint of vanilla coated her tongue. She wasn't sure why her strange ability to read people had also become a magic detector but assumed it had to do with the overall increase in her power and magical knowledge. This felt like a protection spell of some kind, probably to prevent the pages from degrading over time.

Maybe it's part of Scoppic's job to keep the magics on all the books active or topped off or whatever. That would be a mammoth task.

The table of contents informed her that the chapters on poisons lay near the back, so she leafed through until she found it. An index filled the front page of the section, but none of the names seemed familiar. With a sigh, she turned to the first and started reading.

After several hours that brought her not a single step closer to finding a cure for Atreo, it had been time to go to work, time to sleep, time to train, and time to take the new shard to Alessand in the Kemana Stonesreach with Nylotte's assistance. He'd looked at it, given her a wide smile, and told her to return in a few days, when he'd have something to show her. Now, twenty or so hours after she'd entered the library, she had to return to New Atlantis. Her appointment with the Malniets for later that night weighed on her mind as she headed to the Drunken Dragons Tavern.

Zeb held down the fort alone with Janice scheduled to come in to help out in the evening. They exchanged a few words, but he was busy and she was distracted, and the conversation quickly faltered. Invel chose the perfect moment to enter, and they both greeted the Dark Elf. His ashen hair was pulled into a ponytail, which made his handsome face with its patches of lighter colored skin his most notable feature.

"And hello to you two as well." He wore a formal outfit, a black suit over a matching shirt, with a fashionable cane to assist with his limp.

Of course, for all I know, that's an affectation. You can never tell what lengths some people will go to in order to confuse their enemies. That truth was always a good thing to remember, given her deepening involvement in the cesspool of New Atlantean noble politics.

Zeb sounded exceptionally gruff. "Are you headed to New Atlantis with the girl, then?" Cali rolled her eyes. The dwarf knew he was and also the reason behind it. She could never fully understand the relationship between the two of them and only knew they tended to be allied when it came to arguing with the other members of the council.

The Drow smiled. "Indeed so. I've never been there so this should be an interesting experience."

Fyre snorted and she grinned. "Yeah, interesting is a way to describe it. I have a few other words that aren't quite as polite but also apply."

Invel chuckled. "As with all places, doubtless good and bad wage their eternal battle there as well."

"Speaking of battles, it's time we headed out. I need a couple of hours with Emalia before the fight tonight." She hefted the large backpack that contained the gear she'd retrieved from the bunker so it would sit more comfortably on her shoulder. Turning to Zeb, she added, "I should be back for work tomorrow."

The dwarf nodded. "Send word if you can't make it." He refrained from teasing her about Janice—which was a smart move, all things considered. With a short wave, she turned and strode to the basement, trusting that the Draksa and the Drow would follow.

Cali stood awkwardly in the doorway as Emalia and Invel hugged one another. "Is this weird?" she sent to Fyre. "This is weird and it feels weird." He responded with the kind of amusement that left no question that he was laughing at her, not with her.

She stepped forward with a growl. "Okay, you two, break it up. Jenkins, introduce yourself to Invel and show him where his room is."

And if he doesn't plan to stay in it, I do not want to know.

The ghostly presence announced himself and did his trick with the lights to lead the Dark Elf away.

Emalia grinned at her. "Are you blushing, Caliste?"

She shook her head. "No. Whatever. Did you find any more pieces of the sword?"

"No, but I did discover something else useful." She made a motion like a magician plucking a coin from the air, and a charm appeared in her hand. "This one is for creating light. Your intention sets the bar for how much is created, from merely a dim candle to a wickedly blinding glare."

Cali pulled the chain holding her other charm over her head and handed it to her great aunt so she could attach the new one. "Like, permanent blindness?" That was a little more power than she'd be comfortable using under most circumstances.

The other woman nodded. "I think it could be. Again, it's all about intention. You tell it what you want, and it seems to provide it."

"Okay." She accepted it and put it on again, noticing that Emalia had also added another pendant with the shield logo on it. "What's the command? And does this double the shield, or what?"

"No, not double. But the second one will be a good backup for when the first is consumed."

"Smart. Thank you."

Her aunt rewarded the compliment with a small smile. "The trigger word for the light charm is *Iubar*."

She chuckled as it sounded like you-bar, which fit her life fairly well. "*Iubar*. Got it. Does it make a globe or something?"

"No. It merely glows. You'll want to shut your eyes if you use it as a weapon."

"Will do. Fyre, I'll warn you ahead of time." The Draksa nodded and she turned to face Emalia. "Okay. We only have a couple of hours before the fight. I need you to try to teach me a few things."

CHAPTER TWENTY-SEVEN

J enkins had recommended the main ballroom for their training session, to which Cali had replied, "The main what now?" But when he led her to it, she recalled seeing it in passing, although she'd thought it was a formal dining room waiting for furniture. With her current level of knowledge, though, she could easily see how a gathering of the Nine would fit perfectly as the chamber had enough space to accommodate forty or so with ease.

The floor was made of beautiful wood planks polished to a high shine. One wall was entirely windows, and the others were blank. "Was there furniture in here once?" she asked,

"Oh yes," Jenkins replied. "This room was to be redone before your parents were forced to leave. After, with all that had happened, the work was never completed. The items that were removed are in storage in one of the outbuildings."

Emalia nodded. "So that's what I saw. I wondered

where all that was from since it was clearly too big for the place in which I found it."

The lights reached full intensity, and Cali walked into the center of the room. "Okay, we should leave the conversation about home furnishings until later, I guess, or at least not a couple of hours before I have to fight for my life."

Her great aunt followed and stopped a few feet away from her. "What do you want to learn?"

"Lightning." She'd told the older woman about the lightning net she'd faced recently, the lightning line the Malniet had used during the last battle, and her desire to generally be able to use that form of magic. She was comfortable with her control of fire and force and had no interest in learning shadow, which somehow seemed like an evil power.

Of the dark side, it is. She laughed at her internal Yoda voice, exactly as she always did.

"In some ways, lightning is the most challenging power to master, as it requires extreme focus to maintain. Are you sure that's the right choice for you?"

Cali chuckled at the double meaning of the words. "Yes, I'm sure I want to pursue it and yes, I think I'm competent enough to handle the challenge."

Emalia grinned. "Okay, then. Clear your mind."

She went through her mental routine, locked the unnecessary thoughts in their corners, and confined them with caution tape. The process took notably less time than it used to and no longer required her to close her eyes. "I'm ready."

"Imagine your electrical power is something like a

disobedient animal." Fyre interrupted with a growl and they both laughed, and the woman swiveled her head in his direction. "I would never call you disobedient or an animal, Fyre." She returned her gaze to her niece. "You will tell it to do the thing you wish it to do, but the power will strive to do whatever it wants to do when you release its leash—even more than fire does."

She nodded. Her early experiments with fire magic had taught her that lesson well. It wasn't quite alive but definitely had its own opinions on where to go. "Okay. I get that."

"Good. Now, unlike fire—which you can think of as similar to water coming out of a hose—electricity has to be gathered. It's already everywhere and you need to draw the strands together into a point and push that point forward. The lightning will seek to branch out again because that is its nature. You must fight constantly to shape the power into what you need it to be."

"Wait, so you're telling me that the lightning line and net were both magics that required a continuous battle to maintain?"

"That's very well put. Exactly. You'll apportion a part of your mind to maintaining and controlling it. Eventually, that should become second nature. Until then, though, you'll have to be vigilant." She walked to the far end of the room and conjured a transparent wall of force in front of her with an absent wave of her hand. "Now, try to strike me in the chest. Don't worry, my magic will block yours."

Fyre padded quickly behind the barrier and Cali scowled at him. *But he's not wrong given what happened when I tried flame.* The effortless way Emalia used magic showed both her innate talent and her long practice, and she was envious of both. *Okay, here we go.*

She raised a hand and pictured her body as a mass of random electricity, then commanded it to travel down her arm and into her fist. Her flesh tingled as her power responded and seemed greedy for release. She focused hard and held the magic back to force it to slow into a gentle wave that deposited a little more with each surge through the full length of her limb. After fifteen seconds, she felt like there was enough to work with.

"Here goes nothing," she muttered and released the magic, and lightning erupted from her fist. It created an instant Van De Graff generator to go nowhere but make her hair stand on end with its electrical field. She snarled and wrestled with the power to force it to move away from her and form into a cone rather than a cloud. Several minutes passed while she let the power flow and directed it to her will before she was able to maintain a continuous channel of magic aimed at her great aunt's chest. She let it fall and closed her eyes to recenter herself after the internal fight.

Emalia's voice was filled with understanding. "You did well, child. I warned you it wouldn't be easy. This is a bold stride toward your goal, however."

Cali laughed. "But I won't use a lightning whip or anything tonight, either."

"No, you definitely won't. It takes far longer than that to master. But the more you work on it, the more all your magic will improve."

She raised her hand to pat her necklace beneath her shirt. "Well, at least I have a couple of tricks hidden away.

That'll have to be enough. Besides, I can't imagine the Malniets bringing any champions who can stand up to Fyre and I together." With a sigh, she let her desire for additional surprises to spring on their enemies fade. "All right. Let's go prepare, buddy, and get ourselves down to Lutte's."

She'd gathered the items she needed and carried them to the top floor room. Somehow, it felt right to prepare for her battle with the opposing house in the place where her parents had doubtless strategized against them.

Although, maybe not. Coming down that ladder in a dress would be a little challenging. She shrugged and set the thought aside.

Cali removed her comfortable clothes and slipped into the snug combat uniform trousers, tunic, and jacket, then tied the reinforced boots tightly. She bent and twisted to make sure everything felt right before she zipped the coat to her throat. Closing her eyes, she paused, visualized herself in battle, and realized she'd failed to account for something. While the shield charm could be hidden, if the light actually came from the pendant, it would have to be exposed. "Jenkins, please ask Emalia if the light spell requires the necklace to be visible."

"Yes, Matriarch Caliste." A moment passed before he spoke again. "She says that is correct."

"Okay." *Wow, that would have been pretty dumb, Cali. Try to have more brain, please.* She rummaged through the ornamental jewelry drawer until she found another chain, transferred the light charm, and hung it over her jacket. She admired the look in the mirror inside the wardrobe door. The compass symbols stood out in turquoise with red accents, and she looked very serious, as a Matriarch should. The frizzed hair didn't help at all, though.

She found ponytail holders and bound her locks several times into a line that descended the back of her head and neck. A braid would have been more appropriate but there wasn't time for such niceties. She selected an ornamental belt her parents had left and strapped it around her waist. The remaining globe that Invel had provided—filled with wickedly sharp crystals—went into an attached pouch. She stared into the sheaths and shrugged. "Something pointy couldn't hurt, right, buddy?"

"I always have something pointy," Fyre, who had watched her preparations in silence observe. He bared his teeth, and she laughed at the sight.

"That's why Draksa are such fearsome opponents, I guess." He looked pleased with the comment. She snagged two of the sheaths, buckled them around her upper arms, and pulled them tight so they wouldn't slide. Again, she tested her motions and had to loosen the one on her left because it hindered her ability to swing that arm. She slipped the ornamental daggers that went with them into place, and the compass-decorated hilts reached past her elbows. They slid smoothly from their cases and snicked into their sheaths without any problem. After ten practice draws, she knew she could get them into action in only a couple of seconds.

It'll have to be good enough. We're out of time.

With a final pat to ensure her potions were where they

belonged, she led the Draksa down the ladder to the main floor. Both Invel and Emalia waited for her at the front door. They looked at her expectantly, and she tilted her head in confusion. "What?"

Her great aunt lifted her chin and spoke primly. "As the other member of your family currently in residence in New Atlantis, it is both my privilege and my obligation to accompany you to this battle." She grinned. "And he will join us as my escort."

Cali's heart leapt. "Really?" She wouldn't have imagined such a thing would matter to her and was surprised at how much it did. They both nodded. "That's awesome." She snapped her fingers. "Wait here for a second." She raced to the attic room and retrieved two items, then returned. With a grin, she approached her great aunt and pinned the house seal to the collar of the button-down top she wore under her sweater. She did the same to Invel's dark shirt.

Their smiles told her they both appreciated the gesture and approved of the idea. She looked at Fyre, who returned her gaze with his tongue hanging out. "Are you ready to kick some Malniets to the curb, buddy?"

He nodded. "Let's show them why it's a mistake to mess with us."

CHAPTER TWENTY-EIGHT

The walk through the streets attracted more notice than the previous one had, either because she was with unusual strangers or because more people knew of her. Faces turned as they passed and she caught the occasional comment, although they were pitched low and were unintelligible. The person she had been even a few weeks before might have cared. Now, though, that level of worry had been peeled away.

Her focus was on their destination and on what awaited them within. The outer doors of Lutte's were again held open for her by uniformed workers, and she was guided by another to the same waiting room. The attendant inside bowed at her arrival.

"Matriarch Caliste of House Leblanc, Anyas welcomes you back and wishes you good fortune. Are you prepared or do you need a moment?" On her previous visit, Cali had made sure to get there early, either out of respect for her opponent or respect for the venue. She still had some of the latter but lacking the former, had timed her travel down to the minute.

"We're ready. Let's do this." The attendant nodded and opened the door at the far end, which led to a small tunnel that connected the room to the battlefield. The familiar square chamber brought back the memory of defeating Tyrault Malniet inside the combat area delineated by the darker wood in the center of the floor. The two-story ceiling would give Fyre space to fly as long as he dodged the hanging lamps.

She pointed to the lighter wood that ringed the outside of the zone and murmured, "Don't forget to warn them about the light spell and to shield," to Emalia. When her aunt nodded, she concentrated her attention on the opposite doors.

They opened to reveal a swarm of people all dressed in the colors of House Malniet. They fanned out in the viewing area and flowed to both sides. From their midst, a giant of a man, easily close to seven feet tall, stepped forward. He wore plates of armor over heavy chainmail that gleamed silver. Each was etched with an image, rune, or script.

"Holy cow," she sent to Fyre, "I don't think I could lift that chest piece without a spotter, much less wear all that." His emotions in reply were both amused and concerned.

The latter could have been inspired by the creature that walked beside the man. It was easily twice Fyre's size and mostly resembled a leopard in her limited experience. Its base coat was black with spots in rich gold, which made it seem like an expensive work of art that might be on display in a millionaire's home. There was nothing static in the way it moved, however. Muscles rippled under the skin as it padded toward them and it looked like sleek death come to call.

"Are you okay, buddy?" she sent.

A low growl was his reply, echoed immediately by one from the beast. With a shake of her head, Cali stepped forward to her starting position, the Draksa perfectly in step. Their opponents mirrored them. The man's face was hidden entirely by his decorative helm, which reminded her of the statues she'd fought on Oriceran—flat, lifeless, and menacing.

Anyas approached them. Again, she wore a more formal version of the uniform worn by the venue's workers but this time, the long hair that had reached to her waist was piled atop her head, bound by jeweled combs, and possibly required magic to keep it in place. It was beautiful, as was she, but her sharp features made her seem stern and unyielding.

Her voice was husky as she said the ritual words. "House Leblanc has challenged House Malniet. Caliste Leblanc represents her house and has selected a Draksa to accompany her in this battle. Korota Malniet represents his and has chosen a greatcat to accompany him. This is in accordance with the laws of New Atlantis."

A small smile appeared as she faced Cali. "Matriarch Leblanc, do you have anything you wish to say to your opponent?" She offered no reply other than a shake of her head.

Nothing I say now will make a difference. It's up to the Malniet patriarch to end this in any way other than violence.

Anyas nodded and turned to the representative of the

house that had poisoned her brother. "Master Malniet, do you have anything you wish to say to the challenger?"

A deep voice echoed from beneath the helm. "Tonight, you die, girl."

Cali rolled her eyes and commented, "How original. I guess language isn't one of the things their house is concerned with." Fyre snorted and nervous laughs came from Emalia and Invel. The crowd of supporters behind her foes sneered but did not speak. And, of course, the metal face of her opponent betrayed nothing.

The beautiful woman between them backed away until she was on the perimeter, and one of her workers conjured a shield of force to protect themselves and their boss. Anyas called, "Combatants, you may begin."

Cali sent, "I'll work on the metal man, you deal with the animal. If you need to switch, do it and I'll follow your lead." A wash of approval accompanied the Draksa as he vaulted into the air. She had changed her thinking on the Atlantean ritual battles over time. At first, she'd believed staying away from magic at the outset was a tactical advantage but now, she was far more concerned with choosing the best tool for the situation and not worrying about those details.

At this moment, her choice to summon a force shield was inspired when the armored man raised his arms and dispatched twin beams that crackled with confined lightning at her face. Despite the clear mastery of the form that allowed him to keep the wild magic focused, her defense was more than adequate.

She frowned. *That couldn't have been full strength. This jerk is playing with me.* In response, she launched a force blast at his feet, hoping to knock him off balance.

He made no attempt to evade the attack and the bolt struck exactly where she'd aimed it on his right ankle. The rune etched into the armored boot glowed brightly, then faded, and he didn't move an inch.

Uh-oh. This could be a little harder than I expected.

The same thought occurred to Fyre as his first attack on his opponent backfired and almost eviscerated him. He'd gone for the kill, hoping speed and surprise would let him sink his teeth into the back of the greatcat's neck while his foe anticipated him to use his breath weapon. It had seemed perfect until, at the very last instant, the cat rolled and slashed the air with its long claws. A scale ripped away but the rest withstood the assault.

Only because I veered away in time. If I'd kept going, it would have been over fast like I wanted, but not in a good way.

The Draksa wasn't one to worry about past mistakes so he elevated and released a wave of frost over his foe. The cat's quick reflexes made it seem as if his magic moved in slow motion. The creature blurred to the side to avoid the chill attack and sidled closer to Cali.

Oh, no you don't. He dove at it again, searching for options as he closed.

His claws raked down the feline's flank as it darted clear, and he grinned in satisfaction. The weight of it landing on him a moment later drove that positive feeling away. Frye snarled, rolled, and scraped his enemy along the ground to make him release. The tactic worked, but barely. In another second, he wouldn't have had the room to twist and become airborne again. He circled and kept a wary eye on his foe so the cat didn't get any ideas about shifting his attention to his partner.

Okay, what else can I try?

Cali's options were sorely limited. If the man's armor protected him from magic as it seemed to do, half her arsenal had effectively vanished. There was no chance of her magical sticks finding a way through those metal plates, either. She dropped and rolled to the side to avoid the gouts of flame he extended toward her from each of his hands, then bounced up and ran as he tracked her.

I should be able to unbalance him if I can get him to do anything other than ranged attacks. She angled at his ally and he stopped his assault rather than endanger the cat. *Well, that's something, anyway.*

When he fired shadow beams at her face, she'd had enough. He was clearly showing off, trying to get into her head with his mastery of magic, and had begun to succeed. The only option was to quit playing his game. She called a shield in her left hand to absorb and deflect the attack. Again, it felt less impactful than she would have expected. She released her hold on her magic, let it flow through her body to increase her speed, and charged.

She crossed half the distance in a matter of seconds and drove the shield before her to catch his attacks. Without slowing, she snaked her right hand up and drew the dagger on her left upper arm. Whatever opening she saw first—to knock him off his feet with force or finesse or to stab him in a place his plates didn't cover—she'd take it and be happy about it. A grim smile spread across her face as he took a step back.

That's it. Get a little more off-balance, you jerkface, and we'll end this right now.

With only a second left to go, she put her head down and committed fully to bulldozing into him with her shield and transferred all her momentum into one blow to take him to the ground. Unfortunately, the cat struck her and ruined that plan.

Fyre saw what would happen an instant before the greatcat blurred into motion, its incredible speed almost certainly magically enhanced. It raced toward Cali with its claws extended and its sharp teeth snapped, obviously aimed at the back of her neck for a kill strike. He uttered a terrifying screech in the hope that he could distract it and dove for the spot where his partner and the beast would meet. As it collided with her, the Draksa barreled into it and all three combatants were hurled in different directions.

He landed on his side and slid on the slick wooden planks but wrenched himself back to his feet almost immediately. The greatcat was off to his left and Cali directly ahead. He belched a gout of frost at the feline while it shook off the impact. It leapt upward to avoid it and the surface beneath was coated with a sheen of ice. The creature slipped as it touched down and Fyre launched himself forward. The snarling cat regained its footing in an instant, but he already slithered toward it. Another frost blast made it dodge and slip again, and it angled away to his left in an all-out effort to avoid the slippery section of the floor. Most importantly, its trajectory carried it further from Cali.

His path, on the other hand, brought him halfway to the armored figure. The man raised a dispassionate fist and expelled a wide cone of lightning at him. He vaulted immediately to avoid it, but the crackling energy caught him and wound around his body. Rendered immobile, he simply fell and writhed at the biting pain that snuck under his scales. His skin would resist it for a time, but that did nothing to make the agony any less.

With a scream of utter rage, Cali surrendered to the fury inside her, pushed herself off the floor, and attacked the gleaming blank-faced figure who had hurt her friend.

CHAPTER TWENTY-NINE

The armored man swiveled toward her as she approached in a sprint. Cali poured her magic into her muscles to reach him before he managed to turn fully. The lightning attack left Fyre and the blast from his closest hand struck her. The impact was negligible and she ignored the discomfort from the electricity as it licked and bit at her face and hands and chewed at the fabric of her uniform.

She crouched and launched herself at him from a foot away and powered her folded forearms up at his chin. The blow rocked him back and he fell. She landed on top of him and shouted in pain and anger as a sharp edge on one of his armor plates cut a deep gash in her thigh.

Later. There's no time for that now. She hauled her arm back and thrust it forward to stab her dagger into a small patch of skin between the metal collar and the base of the full-head helmet.

A shout issued from within the helm, and she catapulted away with no understanding of what had happened.

She still hadn't worked it out when she landed hard on her backside and slid to scatter the man's supporters. Instinctively, she curled to absorb the impact with the wall. It dissipated the rage that had overcome her and she wrenched her thigh pouch open and searched for the potion within. She lifted it to her lips, opened it with her teeth, and drank it quickly. In ten seconds, she was back on her feet. Unfortunately, so was her opponent.

Fyre surged into flight when the lightning left him, an instant before the greatcat's claws scraped the floor where he'd been. The emotions radiating from his partner were overwhelming and added fuel to the anger that already surged through him. When she was hurled away, he shrieked and flew over the armored figure to bathe him in ice. Every plate his frost breath touched suddenly glowed and when the brightness faded, the man was unchanged.

He banked, swooped past, and used his rear claws to strike the metal warrior on the side of his helmet. There wasn't much behind it, but at least the blow would keep his mind off Cali for an instant. He curved in midair to move toward the cat. He could see what the other creature planned in the way its legs tensed. On another day, he might have avoided the attack and spent more time on the dance rather than risking injury by meeting him head-on.

Not today, though. When the feline leapt with its paws stretched wide to catch him, the Draksa matched his position, fluttered his wings, and positioned all four feet with their sharp claws against the greatcat's belly. He thrashed violently and raked them along the skin while he pressed as hard as he could. The beast screamed and pierced his scales with its claws to draw long bloody lines down his sides. Finally, Fyre's claws punched through and the cat soon began to bleed copiously.

They fell together but the dragon lizard pushed away at the last second and buffeted his wings to avoid a hard landing. His foe pounded into the floor on its side and lay still. As this wasn't his first encounter with a greatcat, the act failed to fool the Draksa. He expelled a cone of frost breath and the seemingly defeated feline lurched out of the way and trailed blood as it positioned itself for the next attack. He'd hurt it and the wounds would surely overcome it eventually, but for the moment, his foe was far more dangerous than it had been.

Cali still didn't know what the man had done to throw her across the room. She assumed it was magical, based on his attacks so far.

Maybe a force wave or something? But it had taught her that even getting into hand to hand combat, where she thought she'd have an advantage, wouldn't be the right answer to the puzzle he presented. *That's fine, I have other options.* She slid up the wall to stand shakily and the calm sense of well-being that always followed a healing potion surged through her.

She stepped forward and punched the air, willing the force blow to strike him in the face. The features on his armor glowed, then faded, and he didn't move. *Okay. I can't punch you with magic because of the armor and can't punch you with fists because of the armor. But thanks to Emalia, I have a trick up my sleeve—or around my neck, to be precise.*

"Another runner in the night," she shouted. It would seem like nonsense to everyone except her allies, Anyas, and the venue's workers, who knew it was both a song lyric and a warning of what she was about to do.

With a shield raised to catch his attacks, raced toward her foe. When she was two feet away, she slid to a stop, squeezed her eyes closed, and twisted her head. "*Iubar,*" she said and held a picture in her mind of an exploding sun from a science fiction movie. As the charm detonated, a momentary hope that the Malniets outside the battlefield wouldn't be permanently damaged was followed quickly by an acknowledgment that they'd chosen to accept the risk by being present for the battle and probably deserved whatever they got.

As unbelievable as it was, she felt the light fill the room like it was a physical thing that swelled around her. It was brilliant against her closed lids, and she was thankful she'd also thought to turn away. A howl of shock turned into a wail of despair from the deep-voiced man in the armor. The magic faded almost as quickly as it had appeared, barely a second's worth of brilliance, and the spent charm fell with a tiny chime.

A crash was followed by a gasp from the crowd, and she opened her eyes hastily. Her opponent writhed and moaned with his armored hands over his helm. A dark shield separated the battlefield from the onlookers, doubtless the venue's doing to protect the spectators from her attack.

I'm glad we remembered to warn them. It had been Invel's idea and she was now definitely in his debt if she hadn't been before.

She twisted toward the Draksa and the cat and lowered her hand to the pouch that held the globe with the devastating crystals. The greatcat was coated with ice, a still statue. Fyre turned to face her and shrugged. "Good job, buddy. Did the light hit him?" He nodded and she sighed. "That's unfortunate."

She walked toward her adversary. "Korota Malniet, do you yield?" Only moans answered her so she knelt beside him and drew her second dagger, the first having been lost somewhere during her cross-room flight. She saw the skin she'd aimed at before but chose instead to use the blade as a lever and pried the faceplate away from the helm.

Beneath it, the man was thin and almost sickly looking, and his unseeing eyes blinked furiously as if that could heal them. He mumbled incoherently.

Damn it. If he can't yield, I'll have to knock him out and given how fragile he looks, it might kill him. She looked at his supporters.

"Healing potion. Now." One of them gave a start, then withdrew a vial from a bag and raised his arm to toss it to her. "Wait," she snapped, then turned to Anyas. "Is it within the rules for your people to verify that it is actually a healing potion?"

The woman nodded and made a small gesture, and one of her associates bustled over and examined it. With a nod, he rolled it across the floor to her. She uncapped it and trickled it into her opponent's lips with one hand, holding the dagger against the bottom of his chin with the other.

His moans faded, and his gaze swiveled toward her. Thank heaven for healing potions. She pushed on the blade slightly, and his eyes widened. Softly, she repeated, "Korota Malniet, do you yield?"

The deep voice had apparently been provided by the magical armor because his words were high and scared. "Y-yes. I yield. Is my cat okay?" She turned to look at Fyre, who licked his paw rather than provide an answer. Returning her gaze to him, she replied, "I'm not sure. Hopefully, you have healing potions that will work on him. He's trapped in ice at the moment." He twitched as if to rise, and she shook her head. "No way. You stay right here until Anyas says it's okay for you to move—long after we've departed. If you and your friend over there ever challenge me or mine again, or if I have even the slightest reason to consider you a threat, you're dead. Do you understand?"

He nodded several times and clearly believed her words. She stood, faced Anyas, and extended a hand to her as the woman walked forward. "Thank you again for the use of your venue. The Malniet family owes you for sparing their followers from the pain of blindness, however temporary." She gestured at her foe's supporters.

Anyas gripped her hand, and the taste of pineapple teased her tongue. She didn't need her magic to sense her goodwill, though. It was clear in her smile and approving tone. "It has been a pleasure knowing you, Matriarch Caliste. I wish you well in all things. If there is any service that I or Lutte's may provide in the future, you have only to ask." Fyre walked up and bumped into Cali's leg, and the other woman laughed. "The same goes for you, noble Draksa."

As they exited with Emalia and Invel talking excitedly behind them, Cali sent a message to Fyre. "One more trick burned. We won't catch them off guard with it a second time. I tell ya, buddy, I'm real tired of this nonsense." The wave of affirmation that swept over her confirmed that his opinion marched hers.

There's no way I'll inch up this damn ladder the way they want me to. There must be a loophole. I merely need to find it.

CHAPTER THIRTY

Her success in the battle against the Malniets would have been the bright point of her week at any other time, but the message from Nylotte telling her that Alessand was ready to show her something exceeded it. She had been given permission to portal to the outer gate of the Kemana but no further, so she pumped magic into her muscles and ran down the tunnel, then down the long staircase that cut through the terraces around the bowl of the city. When she reached the main street, she slowed her pace to a more dignified walk, albeit a very fast one. She was sure that if Jenkins or Emalia could see her, they would have comments about the proper behavior of a matriarch and how she didn't live up to that standard.

Cali didn't care. She only wanted to see what surprise lay in store for her.

Nylotte leaned against the outside of the sword shop, a few feet away from the door. The Drow was dressed all in black leather with her white hair in a topknot. She looked decidedly martial, and the young woman said a small word of thanks to the universe that they were on the same side. At her approach, the Dark Elf stepped aside, opened the door, and gestured for her to enter.

The small showroom of the shop was unchanged from her previous visit. Racks of blades of every type adorned the walls, and the center island was again empty, awaiting whatever the master craftsman would put there. But this time, the door to the back was open, and Nylotte pointed at it. "He's waiting in there for us."

Cali tried to control the bounce in her step as she walked toward the rear of the building. What she found was an almost pristine environment, totally unlike the workspace with anvils, fire, and cooling baths she'd expected. The walls were covered with pale-gray tile, the floor was cement, and a number of long glowing lights above cast their soft illumination over everything and made it seem almost like midday on the surface.

Alessand waited with a wide smile on his face. He wore a simple suit in navy-blue, with polished brown shoes and a white button-down shirt. The effect was more like an investment banker than a sword-maker, but she doubted the former had ever radiated as much pride as the man before her did.

He seemed to barely be able to hold the words back. "I have good news, Matriarch Leblanc."

Quickly, she shook her head. "Cali, remember?"

He chuckled. "Right, Cali. Behold." He waved a hand and a portion of the wall slid aside to reveal two vertical molds of a black material. The one on the left was in the shape of a large sword, with several pieces of metal positioned in their appropriate positions. That was clearly a work in progress as the empty space was more than what was filled. The other, however, was in the shape of a long dagger and held the shard she'd snatched from the Atlanteans. Several other pieces gathered from the bunker were placed near it to create an entire weapon, although still in pieces. She frowned in confusion.

"What is that?"

"That is a present from your parents," Nylotte answered.

She turned to the Drow. "Come again?"

The other woman chuckled. "The final piece was an unexpected bonus, to be sure. But it makes sense that they would have wanted to use it as bait for you as it is part of another blade that has long been in the Leblanc family." She nodded to Alessand. "Do your magic, maestro."

The elf nodded and turned toward the blades. He began to speak, then to chant, and gestured his arms in strange patterns. As he did so, the individual sword pieces glowed and the light increased in intensity with each of his motions. The pressure in the room built and her head began to hurt from the raw power gathering around her.

Finally, with a loud shout, the ambient energy seemed to suck toward the dagger. The individual pieces of metal somehow became solid and liquid simultaneously and flowed into a single, unbroken blade.

Alessand stepped forward and removed it from the mold, then turned and offered it to her pommel-first. She took it and held it up to the light, marveling at the beauty of the etchings and the metal they adorned. "Amazing."

The Drow laughed. "Don't be too effusive. We'll never hear the end of it." She said it with a smile, however and the sword-maker wore one as well. "Now, it took considerable research, but I have determined what the etchings mean and that, more than the blade itself, is what your parents wanted you to have."

Cali stared at them, unable to fathom what message they might contain. Nylotte, of course, would make her ask. She sighed and said, "Okay, I'll bite. What are they?"

The other woman grinned. "You're as easy to irritate as Diana is. How wonderful." She shook her head. "They show the coordinates of a location on Oriceran. And that last rune there—down at the bottom? It's in the local dialect of the area. It means 'treasure.'"

CHAPTER THIRTY-ONE

Ozahl sat in a back booth and looked expectantly at the door. He hadn't been to the Stallion in an age, and the man he appeared to be had never crossed the threshold. His wardrobe was that of a businessman and his face was a duplicate of a tourist he'd seen several weeks before. He constantly searched crowds and stored people's appearances for later illusions and had done so for so long that it was now an unconscious process.

The waiter took his order—Scotch on the rocks for him and cold Prosecco for his date—and he drummed his fingers impatiently on the table while he waited for her to arrive. Danna Cudon arrived a few seconds before the drinks, and he ordered pasta carbonara for them both as she slid into the booth beside him. She looked as stressed as he felt, but his lifetime of pretending allowed him to hide it far better.

She sighed and drank the entire glass before she spoke. "The Empress has been busy. House Jehenel has been drawn into the intrigue and we are expected to increase the pressure on Caliste to join us or end her."

He shrugged. "We knew most of this would probably happen. Why does it have you so agitated?"

Danna shook her head. "You're much better at subterfuge than I am." She laughed darkly. "After all this time, no one even knows your real name although you were part of the gang. I want the girl dead before she can do further harm. I want the Zatoras gone before they kill any more of my people. And I'm tired of the surface. I want to go home."

The mage chuckled. "You may be romanticizing that idea, love. We didn't come from the pretty parts of New Atlantis and in my opinion, New Orleans is far more welcoming. Here, we could live like royalty if that was our choice."

She shook her head. "And you may be romanticizing what our lives here are like. It's different for you as you pull the strings. I am trapped between a multitude of desires—yours and mine, Usha's, the Empress'... If this is living royally, I'd prefer a quiet existence where no one pushed me to do anything."

Guilt flowed over him, a distinctly unfamiliar sensation. She was correct. He hadn't been fully aware of the burden their plans placed upon her.

Well, that changes this very minute. He nodded. "I'm sorry. I didn't see it from your perspective. Soon—very soon—we will have what we've always wanted. A life beyond surface royalty. Nobility in our chosen home, our true home." He took her hands and held them as he continued. "But tell me, what can we do right now to improve things for you?"

The waiter arrived with their food, and there was a pause while they tried it. She ordered another drink, and the server scurried away to fetch it. "There's so much." She sighed. "But truly, probably the best thing for me is to bring the Zatoras to an end. Doing so will allow Usha to flourish, which will take that worry and guilt off my shoulders as well. I'll have additional responsibilities but they'll be clear and manageable in a way that having their threat always snapping at our heels isn't."

He nodded. "Okay. Then that's become our first priority." He grinned. "I expected you'd say you wanted to kill the girl."

A smile appeared on her face. "I assumed you had plans involving her and those might include using her against the Zatoras."

"You are wise, my love." They ate and drank, both in much better moods than when they'd entered. Ozahl's clever mind was already at work on the plan to destroy Grisham and his people. The reminder of his time spent with the Atlantean gang under the identity of Aiden Walsh made bringing down their long-term enemies all the sweeter.

And oh yes, young Caliste will play a key role.

Across town at the Shark Nightclub, the Atlantean gang leader sat at the bar and nursed her third Pina Colada. Her plans for the evening included several more and hopefully, a dreamless sleep in her office. The nights since she'd reported her group's failures to the Empress had been filled with dire dreams and she had woken screaming more than once.

It was clear that Shenni wanted Caliste turned to their side more than she wanted the girl dead. It was evident in her tone if not in her words. And more than anything— even more than the pursuit of her own longing to end the vexatious Leblanc line once and for all—Usha's desire was to give the Empress whatever she wanted.

But how the hell do I accomplish that? What could bring us together in a way that she sees the gang that's tried to kill her as an ally?

As the initiating party, she was able to call the ritual battles off at any time. But if the situations were reversed, she'd interpret that as an insult, a statement of her unworthiness to continue the fight. That's how one of the noble houses would receive it, and Caliste was rapidly growing into her position as matriarch.

No, it's too risky. She would need to request the cessation before I could offer it to avoid that possibility.

One thing she might do was to let word of the possibility trickle out in a way that it reached the girl's ears. That wouldn't be difficult. She set that idea to the side for the moment and considered the larger problem.

Even if she's no longer against us, how do we make it so she's for us? We should have been there for the Kraken attack. That would have at least been a start.

She drained the drink and gestured for another, pleased at how the bartenders lurched into immediate motion. The Kraken issue seemed even more frustrating because she'd done as she was told in that situation as she always did. But she had begun to wonder if the Empress truly understood the position of her representatives on the surface.

I have Caliste on one side, the Zatoras on the other, and the constant pressure to identify a way to rule over the unaffiliated humans when the gang finally rises to prominence. These are all big tasks with enormous risks. With only one wrong move, she would find herself no longer balanced in the middle but alone on one side with the others allied against her. *I can't let that happen.*

She took the new beverage, ate the pineapple and cherry garnish, and tossed the plastic skewer behind the bar. It bounced off the trash can, which was more or less an appropriate commentary on all of her efforts at the moment.

Close but not good enough. She knew the alcohol was making her maudlin, but perhaps that was what she needed—a descent into the darkness prior to finding a way to shoot up again.

Of course, the drugs were her ace in the hole. She could pressure any one of the three groups with the proper manipulation of access to them or activation of the magic within them. The latter was a last-ditch tactic, to be sure, but it might be the right moment to start making those who were addicted less certain of getting their next fix.

And I can blame it on the Zatoras. Or, if needed, Caliste bloody nuisance Leblanc. She stood and stumbled a little, then finished the liquid in the glass and wobbled to her office.

Yeah. It's time to put the screws to them all.

Rion Grisham scowled at his two lieutenants over the remains of the Italian dinner they'd shared. Colin Todd and Jack Strang hadn't complained about the last-minute notice, even though he was sure he'd pulled them away from whatever other plans they might have had. Nonetheless, something this important couldn't wait.

"We have a problem, gentlemen. And, as you've no doubt surmised by the absence of our mage, it has to do with the magicals in the city. Simply put, it's time we ended them. Between the so-called council binding the aliens together and the other gang cutting in on our drug trade, there soon won't be anything left for us. We can't let that happen."

Strang frowned. His sweater bulged over his prominent muscles and his bald head gleamed with a sheen of perspiration.

I probably caught him halfway through a bottle of whiskey.

"How will we do that, boss? I'm down for a battle, whenever and wherever, but it seems they have high-powered resources we don't."

The Zatora leader nodded. "Yeah. That is a problem. So we have to avoid a direct fight."

Todd looked thoughtful and as always, was dressed in a conscious or unconscious imitation of his leader's preference for suits. "So, we'll use guerilla tactics—hit and fade, not a problem. But they'll know it's us, won't they?"

"Most likely. But we can do our best to keep them off the scent. When we go after the council, we'll try to leave enough clues to make it possible it was the Atlanteans, and vice versa. I don't think they're on speaking terms so we ought to be able to sow chaos for a while, anyway."

The bigger man punched his fist into the opposite palm. "Finally. I've looked forward to putting boot to ass on these people for a while. How will you explain it to Ozahl, though?"

Grisham gave him a thin smile. "The first plan is to hope he doesn't notice. If he does, the second plan is to hope he's fooled by the evidence. But if it comes down to it, we'll kill him. Make sure you always carry a weapon loaded with anti-magic bullets. If he even looks at us the wrong way, we shoot first and worry about any fallout later. Got it?"

Both his lieutenants looked deeply satisfied at the possibility of pumping a few rounds into the arrogant mage and they responded in the affirmative.

All right. It feels good to take action. Soon, New Orleans will be ours.

CHAPTER THIRTY-TWO

Cali was happier to be at work than on any other night she could remember. The Tuesday crowd had been raucous and wound-up, and where she might have found that irritating on another evening, it had been a balm to her battered emotions on this one. There was no time to worry about the Atlantean gang, Wymarc Jehenel, Empress Shenni, the Malniets, or any of it. The unending flow of drinks, food, and generally satisfied customers demanded her full attention.

Zeb performed his trick with the soda gun several times and sprayed seltzer at the Rottweiler-disguised Fyre for the enjoyment of those seated around the polished wooden bar. At some point during the evening, Kendra and Tanyith had arrived, but she hadn't had time to greet them. In the quick exchanges of smiles she did manage, they seemed more comfortable with one another than they'd been in the recent past.

She let herself remain lost in the job until the end of the

night when all the patrons were dispatched except for Tay and his girlfriend. Finally, she sat in a chair and Zeb brought a shot glass of hard cider, a full one of soft for her, and tall glasses of the alcoholic version for the others. He lifted his in a toast. "To Caliste, Matriarch of House Leblanc. Long may she remain the person she is."

The others said, "Hear, hear," and they all drank together. She chuckled. "Yeah, well, if I'm to stay the head of the house, I'll need a ton of help. There are battles to be fought, loopholes to be found, sword pieces to recover, and chuckleheads to smack down."

Tanyith slapped the bar. "I'm in for all of it."

Kendra grinned. "I wouldn't be much use in a fight against magicals, but you know you have my support."

The dwarf coughed. "I…uh, have thought about this and believe I'm not doing you any good in the background. Valerie and I will fight at your side whenever you need us."

She had to make a conscious effort to close her mouth after it opened in surprise. "Are you sure?"

He shrugged and gave a small laugh. "It seems like the time when people could safely walk between work and home in this city has passed. I'll definitely be a part of punishing those who took it away in order to help it return. We're in."

"Well then," Cali said, unable to keep the huge grin off her face, "There's no possible way they can beat us. It's time to take New Orleans back and set things right in New Atlantis."

Fyre yawned, a loud affair that took almost fifteen seconds to complete. She laughed and shook her head.

"Okay, it's almost time. We'll sleep first. Tomorrow's soon enough to start taking out the trash."

Cali and Fyre's adventures are far from over and the Atlanteans, Zatora's and others continue to wreak havoc wherever they go. Join Cali and her crew as the continue their battle in Sorcerer's Waltz!

If you enjoyed this book, you may also enjoy the first series from T.R. Cameron, also set in the Oriceran Universe. The Federal Agents of Magic series begins with Magic Ops and it's available now at Amazon and through Kindle Unlimited.

FBI Agent Diana Sheen is an agent with a secret...

...She carries a badge and a troll, along with a little magic.

But her Most Wanted List is going to take a little extra effort.

She'll have to embrace her powers and up her game to take down new threats,

Not to mention deal with the troll that's adopted her.

All signs point to a serious threat lurking just beyond sight, pulling the strings to put the forces of good in harm's way.

Magic or mundane, you break the law, and Diana's gonna find you, tag you and bring you in. Watch out magical baddies, this agent can level the playing field.

It's all in a day's work for the newest Federal Agent of Magic.

Available now at Amazon and through Kindle Unlimited

Thank you for reading the fifth book in the Scions of Magic series! I hope you love these characters as much as I do, and I'm so grateful for the opportunity to keep bringing them to you!

The meme from 30 Rock where Tina Fey says "Wow, what a year, huh?" and Alec Baldwin replies, "It's only February," is really apt at the moment. This has been the longest, most challenge-filled month in recent memory for me. Hopefully it's been easier for you! If you're doing the resolution thing, I hope it's working out the way you want it to. And if it's not, tomorrow is always another day. Give yourself a break.

I went to the Consumer Electronics Show for the first time this year. I've been to big trade shows before, but this one was as crazy as anything. The Uber helicopter just seemed like a bad idea to me, as did the plethora of other autonomous vehicles. I may not be ready for that level of science fiction in real life just yet.

What I am *totally* ready for is the prototype exoskeleton

that Delta Airlines is developing. It will allow a single person to easily lift up to 200 pounds and seeing it in action gave me all sorts of serious Ellen Ripley feels. I can only imagine the applications for medicine, and for other physically intensive jobs.

Season 4 of *The Expanse* was as amazing as expected, and I say this even though the book it was based on was my second-least-favorite one of the eight that have been published. Seriously, watch this show.

My enjoyment of *The Witcher* on Netflix compelled me to buy the first game. It's slow going, as it's over a decade old and the gameplay shows it. But I'm there for the story, and so far that's living up to expectations. I'm looking forward most to Cyberpunk 2077 (by the same studio that produced *Witcher 3*) and the Avengers game, although I hear that the latter might be less story driven than I thought it would be. Hopefully it'll hit the right blend. Plus, for the old school fans, there's going to be a new Baldur's Gate game at some point, which is also the source of many feels for me.

It's looking like we'll wrap up *Scions of Magic* with book 8, so expect excitement galore over the next three books! Not sure yet what's on the docket after that, but as soon as I know, you'll see it in the author notes.

The groundhog said early spring, I think, and frankly it can't come soon enough. Even though we haven't had much winter in Pittsburgh so far this season, I'm ready for summer. The kid and I have four road trips already planned, and I'm hoping to shove another one in there somewhere. Amusement parks galore! I'm very lucky to have someone who likes many of the same things I do.

We've started a daily family game time, since all of us are guilty of spending too much time with screens. We've played a bunch before, but more or less at random. Having an intentional time set aside is turning out to be great fun. First it was Labyrinth, which is deceptively difficult. Then, Catan Jr., which is a fun and easy romp that's pretty dice dependent. Jumping up to Minecraft Builders and Biomes was a pretty big leap, as there are three scoring rounds with different criteria, several different mechanics available in each turn, and an element of luck that can pop up and ruin even the best plans. We're loving it. Next up is probably Ticket to Ride Europe. If you have suggestions for games we should try, please let me know on Facebook!

Until next time, joys upon joys to you and yours – so may it be.

PS: If you'd like to chat with me, here's the place. I check in daily or more: https://www.facebook.com/AuthorTRCameron. For more info on my books, and to join my reader's group, please visit www.trcameron.com.

I know it's the middle of winter for most people right now, but let's talk summer plans. That's what I'm thinking about right now. Maybe it's because in nine days I'll have my first anniversary since I left the day job.

That's right, it's only been just about one year. I was doing two full time jobs up till that point. Even I look back and wonder how I pulled it off. Mostly by not doing much of anything else.

It turns out, setting yourself loose from others' expectations and forming your own day is harder than it looks. I came face to face with my own expectations and habits and found out they have a really loud voice. At first, louder than the one that was new and said, "I wonder what you could do with this day? Are there ways to fashion this so you can work and have some fun?"

That voice got drowned out at first. I did more things, not less. I put more stress on myself, more tasks, not less. It was as if I was getting a sense of self, an identity, from the doing. Doing less, or at least doing it differently meant letting go of that old and useful identity and venturing into a life I had never known.

What do you mean I can do what I want, when I want to? My anxiety was at the roofline.

But, all along I had a couple of other authors – Sarah Noffke and Abby Lynn Knorr who like to post about their vacations in Scotland and their writing spots from Tuscany (Abby Lynn once told me she had to go because her handsome new husband was taking her for a bike ride) – and I would look at those and think, that's what I want. By the way there are far, far, far more posts from authors about how many words they got in on their commute to work or at some wee hour in the morning. Fortunately, all I wanted to say to those were, good for you. No thanks. I admire their diligence and drive but this is where I take a left turn.

But Sarah and Abby Lynn... I want to be them. So, here we are at the anniversary and summer approaches. It dawned on me that I can do one of those daydreams I've had for a long time but never thought would come true. I can go write from a place in Tuscany for a couple of weeks overlooking something beautiful. Maybe vineyards. I can embrace the change and go with the flow and live in the moment.

The Offspring has pointed out that he can watch the dogs so there's no reason not to go. An Italian adventure, and maybe a little research for a few Leira books while I'm at it from a room with a view. Come on summer. More adventures to follow.

OTHER SERIES IN THE ORICERAN
UNIVERSE:

SCHOOL OF NECESSARY MAGIC
SCHOOL OF NECESSARY MAGIC: RAINE CAMPBELL
ALISON BROWNSTONE
THE DANIEL CODEX SERIES
THE LEIRA CHRONICLES
I FEAR NO EVIL
THE UNBELIEVABLE MR. BROWNSTONE
REWRITING JUSTICE
THE KACY CHRONICLES
MIDWEST MAGIC CHRONICLES
SOUL STONE MAGE
THE FAIRHAVEN CHRONICLES

OTHER BOOKS BY JUDITH BERENS

OTHER BOOKS BY MARTHA CARR

JOIN THE ORICERAN UNIVERSE FAN GROUP ON
FACEBOOK!

Facebook Here: https://www.
facebook.com/TheKurtherianGambitBooks/